Intel
15.⁰⁰

YOUR ANGEL ON

BETTER GET YOUR ANGEL ON

STORIES

Alfred A. Knopf

New York 1989

JENNIFER
ALLEN

THIS IS A BORZOI BOOK

PUBLISHED BY ALFRED A. KNOPF, INC.

Published in the United States by Alfred A. Knopf, Inc., New York, and

simultaneously in Canada by Random House of Canada Limited, Toronto. Distributed

by Random House, Inc., New York.

Certain of the stories herein were originally published in *The Quarterly* and

StoryQuarterly.

Library of Congress Cataloging-in-Publication Data

Allen, Jennifer [date]

    Better get your angel on.

    I. California—Fiction.   I. Title.

PS3551.L39385B48   1989   813'.54   88-26904

ISBN 0-394-56867-2

Manufactured in the United States of America

First Edition

BETTER GET

Here's to George's orange trees,
Etty's jasmines, Jenny's couscous,
Lolo's bird, Mister's giggs, Buoy's
ring, Julie's love beads, J.V.'s boat,
Daniel's gospel, Chief's orzata, and
to Richie's our tea dee—big, fat,
gigantic thanks! — JA

Contents

BETTER GET

YOUR ANGEL ON

LIBERATION

This is the night of my life-
time I have been waiting for,
for as long as before I was
ever even alive to be here
now in this two-seat, no-roof
car with bare-chested Trip in
the seat at the wheel beside
me, calling me "My Amnesia
Girl," doing sixty, sixty-five,

seventy down a bent-out-of-whack coastal cliff road, bump-pressed against the belt buckle of the Hitchhiker's leather pants I have been sitting on since the last gas tank fill-up at the freeway detour off-ramp.

The way the wind comes circular to the front, side, back, side of your head, carries Trip's "Amnesia, they are after us!" as the cardboard HELP PLEASE sign of the Hitchhiker flies off the dash into my face and spins out into the dark that is behind us, with no taillights to see where we have come from, with one yellow foglight rope-tied to the top of the metal windshield rim to see where we are going to.

Where Trip, the Hitchhiker, and me are going to looks to me like an earthquake shot through the road; like the sidewalls of a worn tire, the road is cracked in a zigzagged way between the dotted line, with cliff rock and cliff sand fallen down over, turning the two-lane into a zero-lane winding high above the ocean, and even high above the fat white moon that sits way out there at the end of the ocean's long, flat edge.

"Hang on, Amnesia!" yells Trip, and downshifts the no-knob metal stick into my wind-skirted knee, and the Hitch-hiker's gloved hands slide onto skin under my shirt, and the car runs a ramp of jagged cement, catching air in my stomach up my throat, and when the car slams front-fender-first onto the dirt road, the foglight swings loose by the rope onto the hood, spraying yellow this way, yellow that way, and the sound of a dragging fender and of Trip yelling, "Amnesia, we have made it! We have done it! We are definitely free!"

The lights from the speed and gas dials on the dash spot-light Trip's bare chest and beard face, giving Trip to me a look of uneasy green health, so that I am made to think that maybe the button heads the Hitchhiker traded with us for "For a free ride, please" Trip did not have to go ahead and eat them all to himself, the way Trip did right then and there under the flashing arrow sign at the freeway detour off-ramp.

From what I can see by the yellow foglight's this-way and that-way spray, this road looks like a footpath no wider than this car is as wide as my arm is long to push down Trip's doorlock button when Trip sinks his toothy-bearded grip into skin on my arm and the Hitchhiker strap-fastens the seat belt over me and him and my winded-all-over hair tug-catches somewhere behind, maybe in the Hitchhiker's leather jacket zipper or on the Hitchhiker's see-how-you-look-when-you-talk-to-me sunglasses the Hitchhiker had on last I looked, if the sunglasses did not fly off back there into the dark the way the taped-onto-the-dash rearview mirror did.

There is a hubcap rolling along ahead of us down this footpath, the footpath that under my feet under the warm rubber floor is scraping the underside of the car doing thirty, twenty-five, twenty, like all four tires are flat, like the wheels are square wheels, like the entire thing is a coffin taking us down to the ocean.

"Amnesia, watch this!" yells Trip, and the Hitchhiker drifts gloved hands over where my skirt has winded up my legs, and the two wheels on Trip's side skid into the cliff bank, with cliff rock and cliff sand falling into the car, across the dash, over my lap, as the car pitches back onto the path, off the path, down a hill of stones, toward the ocean right there ahead, when—us jerked back by the seat belt—the car jam-stops stuck in the dry ocean sand.

"We have landed, Amnesia! We are here!" yells Trip, and

fits both hands on the metal windshield rim, lifts out of the seat, over the windshield onto the hood; straight on in front of the moon is Trip pushing down and off the shorts that Trip hangs on the tennis-balled antenna bobbing with the engine-run shake, and "Here I go, Amnesia!" yells Trip, and in a swim-crawl move, arms swimming overhead, Trip jumps off the hood, and, through the flattened-moth, dried-shitted windshield, I see bare-bodied Trip under the smeary white moon, fall-running across the sand into the ocean.

The dial lights on the dash go off, go on, go off, and behind my ear my looped earring unloops in a wet trail down my back.

"Amnesia, you guys!" yells Trip. "I can't, I can't touch!"

Another looped earring unloops onto my shoulder and down between to where my stomach is, and there is a sound of water slapping water.

"You guys! Hey, you guys!" yells Trip. "It's pulling me out, it's sucking me off!"

The Hitchhiker takes the car key. The engine-shake stops. Leaning his chest into my back, with my face pushed into the cliff-dusted dash, the Hitchhiker throws the car key safety-pinned to a bunch of car keys (to Trip's bunch of other two-seat, no-roof cars?) into the ocean in a one-dunk splash.

"It's swallowing it! It loves me!" yells Trip.

The Hitchhiker undoes this, there, and here of the buttons on my shirt. I reach back, get my finger in the Hitchhiker's mouth, and reach up higher to the see-how-you-look-when-you-talk-to-me sunglasses that I set on my own eyes and get so much of a just-turned-out-all-the-lights vision that I cannot even see where the moon begins or where the windshield ends, and there is the sound of lap upon lap of water, and the car seat flips me back into a leg-long stretch.

The Hitchhiker unstraps the seat belt from over us and I hear my buttons rip-pop-click on the door or on the windshield or on the dash, and cliff dust is gloved off my knees up to my hips above my legs wide with offshore ocean air coming all around over me now under an unstarred sky so far gone out in black forever—*Amnesia, I cannot believe you have never done a ride like this ever before in all of your life, this has got to be the most only way to ever want to go, to go kicked-back onto your back, pressed against whoever's man chest, hips, hands, sunglassed-blind to the whole entire night.*

THE BURNT

It was at the end of the summer of sunburnt-yellow lawns, of cracked-plastic green garden hoses and salt-watered showers at the beach-side path that the Inland Winds came one night, carrying the fires one house closer to our house, to the neighbor's house that we, the whole entire neighborhood of people I had never before seen so gathered at once, stood in the graveled street, barefooted in bedclothes blowing up and loose in the heated wind, while we watched the neighbor's house burned roof-to-ground, backward from the ground-to-roof way I had watched the house get built taller and wider than any other house in all of our town, to what was now an empty, blackened brush of land where the laddered high-dive and the blue swirl-slide of the swimming pool still stands.

After that night came the last holiday of summer, with my parents and the next-fence-over parents, oiled bodies in swimsuits, air-blown ashes stuck to skin as the parents lounged on the lawn on barbecue-sauced blankets held down against the winds by the jugs of drink the parents were pouring tall ones they drank on from, talking, "That's what happens when you build such a monstrosity of a house, blocking the ocean view from all the other houses here on the block, why such a house anyhow when all you've got is one adopted son who flunks summer school for nailing a shop-class hammer at the principal's nice daughter down the street's forehead, maybe now they'll just have to live on that boat, that *Winded Fever* of theirs they always got parked out in front, they must be out waterskiing the weekend away on, quite a welcome back surprise, wouldn't you say, to come home to, and you think these winds will blow away all that grass seed we just seeded on our lawns?"

I saw my brother and his one-fence-over friend, Judd, walking across the field of ice plant the neighborhood pitched in to have planted as some sort of fire-stopping ivy that had leaves filled with sticky water we kids found lasted longer than any schoolyard chalk you rubbed onto the street to mark the lines for the sides of Nation Ball, New Kids versus Old Kids on the block, we got going every one of those summer nights. When I saw my brother and Judd walking across the field to where the blue swirl-slide stood, I grabbed the nearest hamburger-greased hand of the kid next beside me on the blanket, who turned out to be the New Girl I had slammed flat-faced in Nation Ball the night before my parents kept on telling me to go over say you're sorry to have knocked her two front teeth out. I pulled the New Girl along by the hand with me across the snag-footed ice plant field with the sun straight up above in a cloudless sky, the winds getting the New Girl's unponytailed hair to go into her mouth as she yelled, "You jerk, cut it out!" Coming up on my brother and Judd, I saw the cone-shaped leftovers from The Fourth fireworks in the back pockets of their cutoff shorts, and my brother and Judd, they both started to run that barebacked-boy run with feet kicking up at hind-sides way ahead of me and the New Girl, who was stopping to tie her hair in a high-headed knot.

The New Girl rolled down her knee socks from her street-skidded knees and with a sorry-looking toothless grin said, "So you can throw a ball, so now let's see how you can run," and the New Girl, she took off, fast as she was, to skip-foot the sprinkler heads I got my feet all tripping in a bleeding way on as I caught up to where the New Girl stood at the poolside charcoaled cement patio like another big party barbecue had been going on with the barbecue grill turned upside down, its three legs sticking up, the domed lid off rocking in the wind, red-and-white striped cups floating capsized in the pool's ashed water, and the fanned-branch leaves of the one palm tree skimming along the pool's water where the winds pushed the leaves and a rubber sandal sole into a drifted pile against the tiled edge of the shallow-end steps.

"They're over there!" pointed the New Girl, to where my brother and Judd sat hunched on a black round table that from the middle had a pole going up with wires hooping out in the skeleton of an umbrella, sending spidery sunshadows over the barebacked skin of my brother and Judd. The New Girl's knotted hair fountained in a spray behind as I followed her sneaker footprints that cleared the ash to the table where my brother and Judd had the two Red Devils set up my brother was striking stick matches at that went out fast as they were lit under the cupped hands of Judd.

"Welcome to my palace," said Judd.

Out of her sneaker the New Girl took the HAVE A SAFE 'N' SANE FOURTH lighter the neighbor, who went around claiming himself to be the son of the inventor of butane, had made up by the caseload and told us kids to put one in every mailbox, flag down, on the block if we wanted to get to stand on the roof of his three-story house to see the splattered fireworks shoot up the nighttime sky off all the ocean boats out beyond the canyon in the bay below.

The lighter had a built-in automatic windguard that flipped up when my brother hit the flame on HIGH—and when he set it to the unraveled wick, the Red Devil dudded sparklerlike off, nowhere near how at night far fires across the bay lit the hills gold, the hills that under the sun gave off a gray rising cloud, making the sunsets that summer so large with color we kids would stop a losing Nation Ball game just for us to watch.

"Let me," said the New Girl, taking the last Red Devil.

Said Judd, peeling the skin off the tops of his sun-fried ears, "I've got another house like this one out in San Simeon."

"Let her," I said, "before she goes running home to her mother."

"She doesn't have a mother, all she's got is a hero of a fire-chief father, don't you, huh?" my brother said, tossing the lighter to the New Girl.

The New Girl turned and, one-handedly, "Yep," caught the lighter behind her back.

"Anyone care to join me for a dip?" Judd asked, and kowabunga-ed a cannonball splash the wind blew over us.

The New Girl covered the Red Devil with her I PASSED SUMMER SCHOOL T-shirt she had untied the sleeves of from her hips. Putting the Red Devil on the tabletop, and setting the T-shirt over her head, the New Girl was telling us that this was how it is done.

Judd was climbing the laddered high-dive shouting, "I am God!" loud enough to get the canyon's peacocks going off in their womanlike yelp the way they did every time the fire engines ran through the hills, making you lift the window shade or stand on the roof or turn around to your very own next-door neighbor's house to see how close the fire was or how far across the ocean bay our town's and the next town's over men had to go volunteering to try to put out what an entire county of town's men could not put out to stop.

The New Girl had her head shirted when my brother kneed her elbow to the hand holding the high-flame lighter.

"Daddy!" screamed the New Girl, and shirt sleeves flapped away from her burning hair-knot as she belly-hit the pool water.

"Banzai!" came Judd right onto her bobbing-targeted head.

Both Judd and the New Girl were down under the ash-stirred water when the wind sent the table onto its side and over us came the low-flying spread of a peacock across the pool's waving waters, arcing to land on the tip of the high-dive board where the peacock, feathered wings tucked closed behind the stretch of its neck, cried out into the wind carrying through the canyon. A hand holding a sneaker popped up from the water and then Judd's head and then the coughing face of the New Girl, her shirt bubbled up around her shoulders, her hair now short as my brother's cut short for summer. The New Girl was arming the neck of Judd, who dog-paddled circles, shouting, "This is the life!" when across the ice plant field I saw my parents, Judd's parents, the principal with his baseball #1 SCHOOL IN THE COUNTY hat, and the Butane Neighbor Man with his foot-long cigar in his mouth, running this way toward us kids.

"Act like you're dead!" my brother yelled, and arm-hooked me down onto the patio cement, under the cooled-out shade of the turned-over table, my brother's black-bottom feet next to my face, and Judd pushed the New Girl over onto her stomach to float face down, same as he.

"Thanks for inviting us," I heard my father say.

"Look, honey," Judd's mother said, "a slide!"

"Quiet," said my mother, "you'll wake the children!"

"Geronimo!" screamed the Butane Neighbor Man into the pool.

"Whee!" went Judd's mother, shooting down off the slide into Judd and the New Girl, who were making their way out of the pool, up the chrome-laddered steps.

"Kids!" shouted the principal, climbing the high-dive as the peacock glided down into the canyon of trees below. "Kids! Ever seen a flip swan flop?!" and there went the principal, his hat flying off, ice tumbling out from his tall glass of drink as he ran into the air off the high dive.

"This is wonderful!" my mother said, sitting on the cement at poolside, her feet kicking the water, pouring one more from the jug into a red-and-white striped cup she had gotten out of the shallow-end steps.

"I've been looking all over for this!" Judd's father announced, slipping the rubber sandal sole onto his one missing-sandaled foot.

"What more could you ask for?" asked the Butane Neighbor Man, floating on his back, his sogged cigar in his mouth while my father swam by him with a shark-attack finned-hand cutting through the pool water's leaves and ash.

My brother, Judd, the New Girl, and I, we ran down into the blowing smell of sagebrush, down mounds of dry dirt rock rolling after us, as we went jumping over fallen twisted trees from last summer's fires, over plastic melted shields from winter's landslides, branches scratching at our bare-skinned legs and arms until we came to the man-made trail the fire trucks ran on in the depth of the canyon. The sun was coming down on our beach-burnt skin, and the New Girl, her hair now wind-tossed shagged, said then for us to "Watch!" She flipped the pool-surviving lighter on HIGH and set the flame to the yellow grass that caught quick as hair to fire, and us kids, we took off, barefoot-slipping down the grass toward the blue slate of the always there waiting for us ocean, the hills across the ocean bay giving off smoke clouds, the clouds we said were the Indian call to the Inland Winds, the faraway sound of sirens and the long yelps of peacocks in the onward rush of the wind as we kids pushed, shoved, ran with the all of what was left in the kid of us at the end of our lives that summer.

BETTER GET YOUR ANGEL ON

On Christmas Eve the father
and daughter and also the
lifeguard were all waiting
around the hotel swimming
pool for Mass. The sun had
gone down and Mass would
happen soon like it said it
would on the hotel flyer,
with a live local priest com-

ing in, and red wine, and complimentary wafers included. There was a palm tree with some Styrofoam snow sprayed on it, and the father was standing there next to it, trying to figure out where and how to put on the angel that he had gotten as a free bonus gift along with some sun oil at the hotel store. Its head, the angel's, had BONUS written on it that the father could not seem to get to come off by either pouring sun oil on it or by dropping it into the pool water or by scrubbing at it afterward with the teeth of the daughter's hair comb. And now the father was bending the stalk, and then a branch, and then the stem of a leaf to try to get the rubber wings of the angel onto the palm tree so that BONUS would be facing the hotel wall instead of BONUS facing where the priest would be entering in to begin the vigil beside the light of the swimming pool.

"Could someone please come help me with this?" the father said, and as the father was saying this there was an airplane flying by overhead so that the father could not even hear what he himself was just then saying, and so the father waited, and said, "Please, could someone please come help with this?"

The lifeguard was sitting up in an elevated lifeguard stand, cleaning his beard with the daughter's hair comb. Though the daughter had recently contracted a disturbance of lice, the lice did not so much seem to the father a threat to the lifeguard, seeing how the lifeguard's beard was not grown out of his own face, like the father's beard was, but actually sewn onto a Santa Claus cap that was sewn onto a Santa Claus shirt and additional shorts the lifeguard had been wearing for the entire holiday season or maybe for even longer than that, for all the father knew. This was not all, of course, there was a great deal more that the father knew. For instance, about this daughter here, for instance, who was sitting under the life-guard stand, and who, ever since the sun had gone down the father had noted, had been removing shoe and shoe and sock and sock and then tossing these items into the hotel pool. The father had considered requesting of the daughter that she abstain from this disrobing behavior but did not, after further consideration, proceed with the request, seeing how this was after all Christmas Eve, almost Christmas, and also the daughter's first almost-Christmas with him, the father, and likewise, his with her, the daughter, and if the priest should happen to mention the daughter's untidy demeanor the father figured that he would simply explain that she, the girl, her, the daughter, belonged to him, was baptized a Mary Maria at birth by a bishop, and look at the lovely angel we have placed upon the tree for you, Father. And it was with this thought that the father then said, "Amen," aloud.

"Yo, dude," the lifeguard said, "see that sign? No running, jumping, spitting, yelling."

"Daddy," said the daughter, "you think Jesus was really fucked over so bad?"

Though the father did not applaud the daughter's use of normal vernacular, he did, however, recognize the historic weight of the daughter's question and, further, figured that the daughter was referring to yet another sign, to that of the billboard on top of the hotel which could be seen flashing from where they, the three of them, were all waiting around by the pool, and also seen, as these sorts of signs often are, flashing into the father-and-daughter hotel room both day and evening hours, though most visibly apparent from the freeway where the father had gone walking early this Christmas Eve morning

looking for the daughter when the father could not before find the daughter under the beds in the room or behind the shower curtain in the bathtub or down at the deep-end bottom of the pool or below the hotel store counter, and since this morning's incident the father had made a vow to try to train himself for in the future to look more upward toward Up instead of always looking Down or Behind or Under or Below for any lost or missing matter of concern. The daughter had been, as matters were, all along sitting in the elevated lifeguard stand while the lifeguard was busy being also hotel manager, having to check in a crew of registered guests, some prison-war-soldier-people types the father had figured, noting the leather coats, the leather bracelets around the people's necks, the leather radio the size of a suitcase, and printed on all the people's bald heads L.L.P. with human skulls and crossbones drawn in in tattoolike fashion. At all and any cost, the father, being a father, felt himself responsible to answer the daughter's question, and looking up toward the billboard, seeing " ESUS AVES," and then, "J
S   " on every other flash, the father could only offer to the daughter that this was a vague yet noteworthy example of the mysterious ways in which the Lord does His work, and having offered the daughter this, the father then found himself having to watch the daughter toss her Mary Maria cross and chain into the hotel pool.

"Look, dude," the lifeguard said, "it's the truth, I was there, okay? It was one of those low-flying seven forty-seven hijacker jets that fucked that Jesus up for good."

The father was watching the cross and chain, how the underwater light of the pool touched upon it, making the cross and chain look to the father like a falling, not a shooting, star, a distinction of which the father then determined at this exact moment, that there were two types of stars, one which shot up into the universe, and one which fell down toward the earth, and this was but one of a series of celestial thoughts that the father had had which he did not feel, or at least not at the present time, accountable for to have to discuss with the daughter.

"Daddy," the daughter was saying, "Daddy, Santa says me and him can go get married, make babies soon when we want."

"What?" the father said. "I'm what?"

"Yo, dude," said the lifeguard, "better get your angel on before the priester shows, you know how pissed priesters get over angels off."

The father then looked at the angel he had been holding on to for all this while while waiting for Mass, and saw that the clarity of BONUS had been altered on its head, so that now the angel's head had an imprecise roam of black on it, and the hair that was before white threads was now black as well, and so was the father's palm of his own hand black, and the rubber wings of the angel seemed to the father to be bent forward around the angel's breast. The father thought that he, being a father, should correct this physical inaccuracy by taking the wings with his teeth and then bending the torso with his hands, which he did do just then, and when doing so, the father heard music, music of the kind which the father had earlier this morning heard in the hotel lobby when he had had to ask the prison-war-soldier-people types if they would not mind altering the loud mortality a tad so that he could speak instead of having to shout to the hotel manager about the loss and missing matter of the daughter.

SEA GIRLS AND MEN WITH HANDS

Winter Sundays at Boneyard Cove you can come see the fishermen's women, how these women sit with blanketed shoulders on fold-up wooden chairs set along the rocks at low tide where the white salt waters hit the barnacled hull of the

"Too late, dude," the lifeguard said, dropping the hair comb down to the daughter.

And the daughter was pointing, and screaming, "Look, Daddy, look!"

The father looked up and saw that there on the other side of the swimming pool came three, the father counted, three men or women or counterparts of both, the father was not exactly sure, though the father was sure, by the sound of what looked to the father like an exhaust pipe the first person was blowing on and also by the sound of a trash-can lidlike–looking thing this person was banging up against the side of his or her or counterpart of both head, that these were certainly the same prison-war-soldier-people-type guests who had earlier checked in, seeing how there were not many people, if any, whom the father had seen living at the hotel, and also none of whom the father had ever, however casually, known to be so uniformly bald, and with so large boots for feet, and with also so great an aroma of leather on such a temperate eve as this. Seeing these people follow behind the person blowing the exhaust pipe and banging the trash-can lid, the father figured that these people were following as in a procession to take the body of Christ, Amen, and how remarkably true it was that the followers of Christ do come in all forms of human life, and perhaps one of these people would help with the straightening out of the angel wings which the father was then examining and saw that the wings now had teeth bites, and the father thanked God that he was himself just a father and not God who might be relied upon for having to make an angel such as this one fly.

"And now," the lifeguard yelled, "the priests you've been

waiting for, you knew them as The Dead Agains, and now, back by popular demand, let's welcome, Live Local Priests!"

What was to the father a procession broke, and the one with the exhaust pipe and trash-can lid went on blowing and banging and walking, and another bald one was swinging a bottle and drinking from it and then was pouring what looked to the father like red wine onto the daughter's head, and the daughter was clapping her hands and kicking her feet in the water of the pool, and another man or woman or counterpart of both was walking his or her or both boots up to the father and picking up the palm tree and then throwing the palm tree into the pool, and there was an airplane heard flying by, and the lifeguard was shouting, "On, Dasher—On, Dancer—On, Comet!" and here was the father wondering about this angel here and what could be done with now the palm tree more or less sinking into the pool, for the father did indeed think about this, about the pool and the angel and the palm tree and the cross and chain being somewhere down there too, and the father wondered if there was ever on this earth an underwater Christmas Eve Mass.

"Who's got the food?" someone yelled.

And someone else yelled, "Who farted?"

And the lifeguard yelled, "Shit, you girls planning on getting paid or laid for this?"

And though the daughter was, by now, taking off her shirt and then taking off her shorts, and though the Santa Claus cap and beard and shirt and additional shorts were being tossed into the pool along with some leather brassiere and leather underwear of the counterpart sitting in the lap of the lifeguard up in the stand, and though also the bottle was being broken

onto the pool patio, breaking glass in with daughter was combing her hair comb through at, the father still somehow knew that the most of all of the Lord's work so far this Christmas Eve fact that here stood a father, and the father, well, not the father then take it upon himself, or no, wit the father thought, take it within thyself to perform of Mass? Did it not, in the end of all ends, come p that, to this, thought the father, that I am the father.

And so the father began. Beginning by announci that Mass would be held momentarily, thank you, and holding the angel held in both hands, the father walked a the pool patio, to the pool steps, and into the pool itself, though this walking through water seemed so slow to the ther, the father knew that this was after all a procession to ho or the birth of the son of God, and that this required th slowest of all reverence as was reverently possible, and with this understanding in mind, the father maintained the formidable step-together-step-together steps, and looking up as the father had vowed to train himself to do, the father was then noting how the pool floor was descending now too, with everything going down to get up.

fishermen's boat, the *Sea Girl*. These two women, the two of what winter storms back were three women who came here, I saw the day after the fishermen's boat ran the jut of rocks, how these three women swam out into the turning waters while the coast guard air-horned of riptide undertows, how these women kept on until one and then another came treading in a crawl back onto the rocky shore, the first carrying the torn flag of the *Sea Girl*, the second a knotted fishnet, and the third, this woman, she was lifted by rope out of the waters onto the coast guard's boat as it motored waves away out of Boneyard Cove.

This Sunday, today, after an all-night foghorn/foglight every hour on the half-hour watch, I walk the dirt path down the cliff to Boneyard Cove, sit myself down behind the fishermen's women's chairs, close enough so the offshore mist moves the flowery taste of perfume my way, close enough so as to hear the woman who has the *Sea Girl* flag scarved over her hair say, "Sure as this is Pacific, my Bill, he is still out there, I am sure of it. Bill is out there on that island, being fed homemade mayonnaise by a native beauty with hair down to her heels, under the shade of a coconut palm."

"Island, what island?" the other woman says, unknotting the fishnet that covers her legs. "There hasn't been an island out there for years."

"Oh, it's out there," the scarved woman says, the woman who now stands, the blanket dropping off her shoulders onto the chair. "It's about right over there." She points. "You just can't make it out so well through all this haze."

"You're the haze," the other woman says, unknotting the fishnet with her teeth. "Walk around with that flag on your head, do you know that is authentic hand-dyed silk imported back from Fiji by Jim himself? You could make a good dollar or two selling it at the pier bazaar instead of waiting around the dock mailbox how you do every day waiting for your monthly check."

Today the fog banks in low to the wishbone curve of Boneyard Cove. A daytime fog with the sun somewhere above, barely burning through, making your eyes weak to the morning glare. You cannot see beyond the end of the rocks where the swelled waves come in, where the waves rise to hit the *Sea Girl*'s red-painted hull, salt-worn to a red sort of brown, the brown of the kelp beds that float with the weight of a gull landing there, chewing on a piece of what looks like plastic bag.

"Maybe you're right," the scarved woman says, pushing her sunglasses off onto her head. "Maybe Bill is out in Fiji now, speaking Fijian with the native women dancing around his feet, Bill eating roasted pig from an open fire. It must be night in Fiji. Don't you think it's probably nighttime there in Fiji now? And Bill, I can see him laying his tired back down to rest on a bed of palm leaves."

"Did I tell you, last week's bazaar I made twenty plus off those broken brass barometers Jim had hanging out on the porch?" the other woman says, pulling the chopstick out of her tied hair. The woman's hair drops a sun-bleached grayish blond over her shoulders as she goes at the knots with the chopstick, saying, "When this is done, it will make a hammock for seven or eight easy."

Eight dollars per half-hour watch is what I get for staying awake while standing up, for not falling over and waking with my face pressed against the handled controls, the foghorn/foglight both turned to a flashing OFF in the midst of a night

"Too late, dude," the lifeguard said, dropping the hair comb down to the daughter.

And the daughter was pointing, and screaming, "Look, Daddy, look!"

The father looked up and saw that there on the other side of the swimming pool came three, the father counted, three men or women or counterparts of both, the father was not exactly sure, though the father was sure, by the sound of what looked to the father like an exhaust pipe the first person was blowing on and also by the sound of a trash-can lidlike–looking thing this person was banging up against the side of his or her or counterpart of both head, that these were certainly the same prison-war-soldier-people-type guests who had earlier checked in, seeing how there were not many people, if any, whom the father had seen living at the hotel, and also none of whom the father had ever, however casually, known to be so uniformly bald, and with so large boots for feet, and with also so great an aroma of leather on such a temperate eve as this. Seeing these people follow behind the person blowing the exhaust pipe and banging the trash-can lid, the father figured that these people were following as in a procession to take the body of Christ, Amen, and how remarkably true it was that the followers of Christ do come in all forms of human life, and perhaps one of these people would help with the straightening out of the angel wings which the father was then examining and saw that the wings now had teeth bites, and the father thanked God that he was himself just a father and not God who might be relied upon for having to make an angel such as this one fly.

"And now," the lifeguard yelled, "the priests you've been

waiting for, you knew them as The Dead Agains, and now, back by popular demand, let's welcome, Live Local Priests!"

What was to the father a procession broke, and the one with the exhaust pipe and trash-can lid went on blowing and banging and walking, and another bald one was swinging a bottle and drinking from it and then was pouring what looked to the father like red wine onto the daughter's head, and the daughter was clapping her hands and kicking her feet in the water of the pool, and another man or woman or counterpart of both was walking his or her or both boots up to the father and picking up the palm tree and then throwing the palm tree into the pool, and there was an airplane heard flying by, and the lifeguard was shouting, "On, Dasher—On, Dancer—On, Comet!" and here was the father wondering about this angel here and what could be done with now the palm tree more or less sinking into the pool, for the father did indeed think about this, about the pool and the angel and the palm tree and the cross and chain being somewhere down there too, and the father wondered if there was ever on this earth an underwater Christmas Eve Mass.

"Who's got the food?" someone yelled.

And someone else yelled, "Who farted?"

And the lifeguard yelled, "Shit, you girls planning on getting paid or laid for this?"

And though the daughter was, by now, taking off her shirt and then taking off her shorts, and though the Santa Claus cap and beard and shirt and additional shorts were being tossed into the pool along with some leather brassiere and leather underwear of the counterpart sitting in the lap of the lifeguard up in the stand, and though also the bottle was being broken onto the pool patio, breaking glass in with red wine that the daughter was combing her hair comb through and then licking at, the father still somehow knew that the most least mysterious of all of the Lord's work so far this Christmas Eve was the basic fact that here stood a father, and the father, well, then, should not the father then take it upon himself, or no, within himself, the father thought, take it within thyself to perform the service of Mass? Did it not, in the end of all ends, come precisely to that, to this, thought the father, that I am the father?

And so the father began. Beginning by announcing to all that Mass would be held momentarily, thank you, and then, holding the angel held in both hands, the father walked across the pool patio, to the pool steps, and into the pool itself, and though this walking through water seemed so slow to the father, the father knew that this was after all a procession to honor the birth of the son of God, and that this required the slowest of all reverence as was reverently possible, and with this understanding in mind, the father maintained the formidable step-together-step-together steps, and looking up as the father had vowed to train himself to do, the father was then noting how the pool floor was descending now too, with everything going down to get up.

SEA GIRLS AND MEN WITH HANDS

Winter Sundays at Bone-
yard Cove you can come see
the fishermen's women,
how these women sit with
blanketed shoulders on
fold-up wooden chairs set
along the rocks at low tide
where the white salt waters
hit the barnacled hull of the

fishermen's boat, the *Sea Girl*. These two women, the two of what winter storms back were three women who came here, I saw the day after the fishermen's boat ran the jut of rocks, how these three women swam out into the turning waters while the coast guard air-horned of riptide undertows, how these women kept on until one and then another came treading in a crawl back onto the rocky shore, the first carrying the torn flag of the *Sea Girl*, the second a knotted fishnet, and the third, this woman, she was lifted by rope out of the waters onto the coast guard's boat as it motored waves away out of Boneyard Cove.

This Sunday, today, after an all-night foghorn/foglight every hour on the half-hour watch, I walk the dirt path down the cliff to Boneyard Cove, sit myself down behind the fishermen's women's chairs, close enough so the offshore mist moves the flowery taste of perfume my way, close enough so as to hear the woman who has the *Sea Girl* flag scarved over her hair say, "Sure as this is Pacific, my Bill, he is still out there, I am sure of it. Bill is out there on that island, being fed homemade mayonnaise by a native beauty with hair down to her heels, under the shade of a coconut palm."

"Island, what island?" the other woman says, unknotting the fishnet that covers her legs. "There hasn't been an island out there for years."

"Oh, it's out there," the scarved woman says, the woman who now stands, the blanket dropping off her shoulders onto the chair. "It's about right over there." She points. "You just can't make it out so well through all this haze."

"You're the haze," the other woman says, unknotting the fishnet with her teeth. "Walk around with that flag on your head, do you know that is authentic hand-dyed silk imported back from Fiji by Jim himself? You could make a good dollar or two selling it at the pier bazaar instead of waiting around the dock mailbox how you do every day waiting for your monthly check."

Today the fog banks in low to the wishbone curve of Boneyard Cove. A daytime fog with the sun somewhere above, barely burning through, making your eyes weak to the morning glare. You cannot see beyond the end of the rocks where the swelled waves come in, where the waves rise to hit the *Sea Girl*'s red-painted hull, salt-worn to a red sort of brown, the brown of the kelp beds that float with the weight of a gull landing there, chewing on a piece of what looks like plastic bag.

"Maybe you're right," the scarved woman says, pushing her sunglasses off onto her head. "Maybe Bill is out in Fiji now, speaking Fijian with the native women dancing around his feet, Bill eating roasted pig from an open fire. It must be night in Fiji. Don't you think it's probably nighttime there in Fiji now? And Bill, I can see him laying his tired back down to rest on a bed of palm leaves."

"Did I tell you, last week's bazaar I made twenty plus off those broken brass barometers Jim had hanging out on the porch?" the other woman says, pulling the chopstick out of her tied hair. The woman's hair drops a sun-bleached grayish blond over her shoulders as she goes at the knots with the chopstick, saying, "When this is done, it will make a hammock for seven or eight easy."

Eight dollars per half-hour watch is what I get for staying awake while standing up, for not falling over and waking with my face pressed against the handled controls, the foghorn/foglight both turned to a flashing OFF in the midst of a night when a winter storm throws water down from the sky and up from the ocean in waves tall enough to clear a bait shack off the end of pier, tall enough to knock away years of standing wood-pier pilings out over the beach sand and through the windows of beachfront homes.

The scarved woman takes off her sunglasses, rubs the lenses with a ragged end of the *Sea Girl* flag, and slides the sunglasses back onto her head. "Bill," she says, "that tropical sun must be murder on his eyes, a whole day out on the boat and Bill's eyes get so bloodshot red that they actually look greener, like green as, even like, well, those fish—you know those fish we got the extra freezer for? Like green as those fish bellies are, if you can believe it, Bill's eyes, I've seen them look just as green as that."

"You think if I got this wet, any of this mess would come out any easier?" the other woman says, placing the chopstick behind her ear. "Jim used to say, what did he say, something about how water makes the hardest work easy—something like that. I can't remember it now, can you?"

I can.

I can remember how these three fishermen I saw from my tower window came walking up the stone steps on a day when there was sun so wide and far for miles that you could see all the way out to where the ocean ended in a mountain of island. These three men walked side-to-side in a heavy wet-boot way up the stone steps to the door down below, calling out, "Knock, knock, anybody home?" I went running down the spiral stairs, lost a beach sandal along the way, to unbolt the double-iron triple-bolt doors. And opening up, "Christ," said the one with sunglasses on, "got enough locks to hold out a whole drunk ship of navy." "Can we come in?" said the other, wearing a *Sea Girl* windbreaker, as the third one walked in, stepping wet on my bare foot. This third one ran the spiral stairs, soon out of sight, and the one with sunglasses ran after him, shouting, "Hot on your wake! Hot on your wake!" "Jim," said the one with the *Sea Girl* windbreaker, putting out his hand that went what felt like two hands around mine. "The boys here, as you can see, are a bit excited. None of us has ever gone in a real-life lighthouse before. Mind showing us how you work the ropes here?"

So what ropes are there to show of the two-handled controls. What is there really to show to these fishermen, to these men with hands. I watched one by one each take a pull at the foglight handle. Here were hands built bone-strong to reel, net, lift a deckload of flapping fish, hook-cut hands through storms of winter, lightning nights of spring, red-tide deadfish days of summer, and through the fall when the winds turn the currents oceanward; hands that worked these men a way to feed a beach town for more years than I have been alive. And what do you say when the one with sunglasses on throws an arm around your neck, pulls you close to his freshbait smell, and says, "So you're the mighty lighthouse king," while the third one, with his head out the tower window, asks, "Ever think of jumping?"

As I followed the fisherman called Jim back down the spiral stairs, he said to me, "If you want to come out on the boat sometime, do." And then at the iron door, when the other two men were running on ahead, this man, Jim, he said, "You know, son, it's good to see someone as clean-cut all-American as yourself—though you're missing a shoe, you know—is up here watching over all us boys down there in the water. You keep up the good work, now," and then Jim gave me a big-handed slap to my shoulder and made his side-to-side way slow down the stone steps.

Fogged days such as this, you can tell time by how high the waters come up over the rocks, how far the waters now cover the slanted deck, burying the *Sea Girl* on the bow, making the time somewhere between an hour or less left of day, making also less of a walk from the women's chairs to the water's edge, where the other woman goes dragging the fishnet behind, the fishnet that catches on rocks here and there as the woman keeps on walking, giving a tug here and there until she reaches the tide-pool waters. There she bends, her hair falling over her face as she dips, draws the fishnet in, out of the water, while the scarved woman, she moves back to her wooden chair, pulls the blanket over her shoulders, sits.

"Look here!" shouts the other woman, carrying the fish-net dripping over the stomach of her dress. She lets the fishnet unwind onto the rocks, and there caught within the net are needled sea urchins.

The scarved woman takes a sea urchin by one of its nee-dles, drops the urchin onto the rocks, where the needled shell breaks, and, leaning over out of her chair, says, "Bill loves these. You get the egg here, scoop it out like this, and taste."

"No, thanks," says the other woman. "I'm saving mine. I can get five flat a pound off these at the fish market."

"Maybe you're right," says the scarved woman, wiping the egg into the shell, "maybe I should save mine for Bill."

As for me, the mighty lighthouse king, I saved no one in my standing sleep on that winter-storm night when not even the coast goard boated out, a night the navy halted all shell practice at the island after what years of calm winter has left a strip of sand that disappears down under at high tide, a night the soundless thick of fog comes in around you, waiting for your half-hour duty call to no one out there anyhow, you think, until the afterstorm of the next day, when you, or I should say I, when I saw the one boat of the only fishermen I knew in this entire beach town I grew up in is rock-wedged in the point of the cove below. And maybe, I thought, maybe they're not on it, maybe those three fishermen did not tie the boat up tight to the docks, maybe the boat got shoved loose by the storm and drifted out on its own into the night. But I knew there was no possible way those fishermen's hands would miss-dock the boat that gave them their ocean living they worked for to have to their very own deaths.

"It's about that time," the other woman says, gathering the sea urchins into the knotted fishnet.

"Yes," the scarved woman says, "I've got to get this in the freezer."

And these women, they take hold of their blankets with both hands, press their chins to the center of the blankets to fold once, drop twice over their legs, and then place the blankets in the seats of the wooden chairs they close, and I follow. I follow this one with her chair under her arm, the fishnet slung over her shoulder, and this one, this one with the chair held on her scarved head, up the dirt cliff path of Boneyard Cove to the grassy mound of uppermost land, where I stop.

I stop and watch these two women toss their chairs, and then this one her fishnet, into the flatbed of a truck, where two men sit in the front cab, harpoons hung in the rack behind their black-capped heads. These women climb in through the opened cab doors, over the men's laps, to a shoulder-to-shoulder seat between the two men, who shut the cab doors, and when the engine starts up, the scarved woman slips the *Sea Girl* flag down off her red-gold hair, and SKINDIVERS DO IT DEEPER on the bumper as the truck drives in a dirt cloud away.

Here is the *Sea Girl*'s rusted anchor sunken in the grass where I saw, winters back, these same two women throw dust over their shoulders off the cliff to the waters of Boneyard Cove, dust that could have been dust of anything but of the fishermen who to this day are somewhere unfound, out there under the waters that cover the hull of the *Sea Girl*, where gulls waver above, and where now, as on every winter Sunday at this hour at Boneyard Cove, you can see the sun coming through in a fog bow of light—me standing, looking out to the who-knows-how-deep of the ocean's waters to where there are those who are lost at sea, from this point here where there are the those of us who are lost on land.

1987

It is New Year's Day on the strand and I am watching a man who has blood on his face that looks to me like the blood is coming out of his eye give one, two, three kicks to the stomach of a woman who is on her knees in a puddle of sand under an outdoor shower that is on when a kid wearing a hat that says HAPPY NEW YEAR in glitter with palm trees sticking out of both sides slaps my ass and asks whose blood I think all that is messing up the sand, his or hers. "Hard to say," says I. "Nice hat." "Pilfered," says the kid, "thanks," and the kid slides a fat one out from a palm tree, holds fat one with kid lips, tokes up by match.

The shower has the dress the woman is wearing hug the woman's thighs, stomach, and "Nice tits," says the kid, and the kid fingers the fat one over to me.

The man flips out a "Stiletto, rad," says the kid, and the man holds the stiletto with both hands the way and the where a man holds his pisser.

The woman goes down on her stomach, holds the man's ankles, and it looks to me like the woman is biting one of the man's ankles. "No," says the kid, "she is trying to give head." I finger the fat one over and the kid elbows me. "Go show her," the kid says, "how to give head."

"If I knew how I would," I say, and "No shit," says the kid, "you wet-lipped this one limp." The kid takes a toke, juts kid jaw, and out of kid mouth comes one smoke loop and then another that floats right through the one.

The man lifts the ankle the woman is trying to give head to and the man moves his leg in a kick and the woman goes back on her back into the puddle. The woman starts to throw sand and the sand hits the man's face and "Ew, shot to the eye," says the kid. The man wipes eye with back of hand holding stiletto and the woman, "On a comeback," says the kid, stands.

"Toke or pass!" says I, and the kid takes a long drag and blows long drag in my face and with kid smirk fingers what is left of fat one over to me.

I bite off the wet limp end and spit it at the kid's hat and the kid says, "Fucking wild, check it out."

The woman has inside of both legs around outdoor shower pole and with hands, feet, and legs the woman goes up the pole. "Jerking off for a good douche," says the kid. "Could be," says I, and the butt of the fat one goes out and I chew and swallow.

The man does not have the stiletto. "It's in the sand, there," points the kid, and the shower makes the blood and sand on the man's face go down the man's neck and the man lifts one foot, puts one foot on shower turner-on-er and the man pulls the woman's dress and the woman's dress rips. "Nice," says the kid, and the man holds the ripped dress in his mouth and pulls the woman's foot, and the woman and the man go down, "Kerplash," says the kid, into the puddle.

The man stands, puts one foot on the woman's stomach, and the man unzips the pants the man is wearing and pulls his "Kamikaze yang," says the kid, out of his pants and the man pisses on the woman and I ask the kid if the kid has any more grass and the woman reaches up and holds the man's kamikaze yang and I start to tear apart kid's palm leaves in search of one more fat one and the kid takes hold of both my hands, puts both my hands behind me, knees kid knee in my back, says, "If you want to know how it's done, look." The woman has her mouth and one hand on the man's kamikaze yang and the woman has her other hand reaching for the stiletto and "Look out!" screams the kid, and the woman puts the stiletto into the man's thigh and I bend over fast and the kid goes over my back and into the sand. "Back off, bitch," says the kid when I go to help kid back up, and now the woman is on her stomach on the man's stomach and the stiletto is in the man's hand and there is blood all over the man and the woman and the puddle of sand and the kid says, "Mom and Dad, they are so in love," and "No way," I say, and "Yes way," says the kid, and the kid starts to laugh kid laugh with kid face.

The kid gets up and puts on HAPPY NEW YEAR hat with palm leaves torn apart and "See ya," says the kid, and the kid walks away. I run after. "Wait!" I say. "Where are you going to?" and "Sorry," says the kid, "I do not hang with lightweights who Do Not Know How." "It is New Year's Day," I say, "there has got to be a party we can go find somewhere along this here strand." "New Year's Day," says the kid, "that's tomorrow, babe," and the kid puts kid hat on my head, gives me kid wink, says, "See ya, babe, later days."

ISKOMAN

No one saw the Indian break
the branch off the tree, strip
leaves off the branch, tie
cloth brown with blood of
snake to the unbroken tip of
branch, take hold in one
hand the branch and run.
No one saw the Indian run
long with legs through the

water and the rock that streams down between hills of tall grass, between fence rails of lying cattle, run down easy in breath to where water, rock, grass end at ocean. Run here, where the Indian stakes the branch deep into the wet of the low land, and so remains, in the rise of the moon after, the brown cloth tailing back toward the grass hills, toward the trees in the winds of Coho.

Jalama. Jalama Ranch—that is, to the Cattleman who sleeps in a cabin built of the same lasting wood that fences in a day-by-day lesser herd of cattle. A cabin with a cot stuffed with bird feather, with an iron stove that burns the dry sticks that cover the high lands, with a coyote leg with paw to scratch at his sun-dried back after a day out on saddle. A day when the heat of the sun softens the reins the Cattleman tugs to lead the horse past a drink of stream, past a coil of snake, palms brown with the day-long wear of leather, of hides of cattle once many enough to have fed the grass off the hills to a thin dirt, back then when the Cattleman, before sleep, kneeled for rains to come. Now kneels to no one. Sleeps as the coyote chews the supper meat dished in the brush outside of the cabin.

Yet far from the cabin, far out along the fence rails, come two more, come John and Jill on foot. John, compass hung from around his neck, holds flashlight to swollen eyes of lying cattle, to PC brand burn on cattle's balding rumps, and to Jill, Jill with poppies woven down along her braid of hair.

Says John, "PC, Point Concepción—we must be here."

Says Jill, "I could think of better honeymoons."

"Jillie Bug," says John, taking then who other than Jill into the pull of his arms, his hips to her hips, compass pressed to

their breasts, dropping flashlight onto grass, where it lights on
TRESPASSERS WILL BE SHOT HANGED KILLED nailed to the
fence.

"Jillie Bug Queen," says John, "tell me, so help me, tell it to
me just this once more, say I do."

From where these two, John and Jill, stand, the moon cannot be seen, has not risen above the grass hills they have walked
down from, the pine trees they have walked under in the high
lands, where now, by hands and feet, moves the Indian up the
tree to a branch twice the thickness of the Indian's thigh. Here,
the Indian sits under a half-dark moon, pulls pine cones off the
branch above, picks pine nuts, eats. When onto the Indian's
calf comes snake, Indian takes snake by its neck, bites skin,
drinks. An Indian, no less, who sits toward the winds, toward
the grass hills, toward the cabin in the low lands.

Outside the cabin, coyote drinks last of water and last of
grass out of horse bucket, lifts its snout and yowls out into the
night. The horse tied there to the porch post dips its head,
hooves the bucket. Cattle bells from the hills. Frog burps from
the stream. How could any man sleep? The Cattleman takes
the pistol from under the cot, spits bird feather, cocks the pistol
and, aiming through the crack between windowpane and loose
hinge, fires. Hits. Blood of coyote on horse's blond chest, on
horse's mane.

"What was that?" says Jill, Jill with naked length of body in
damp of tall grass while John here tongues poppies out of
braid of Jill's hair.

"Did you hear that?" says Jill, and Jill, she yanks braid out
of John's mouth, sits herself up, hands the grass, the compass,
the buttons on the dress.

"Flashlight!" says Jill.

"Ate it," says John, and this John, he draws this Jill by her braid onto his chest, slips a leg over.

"Jesus, Jill," says John, "you taste like, like I don't know, like Jesus, God, Jill."

Now next day follows, as days do follow nights such as that one prior, and on this particular day at Point Coho Jalama Concepción Ranch, the sun has risen up beyond the pine trees, up beyond the grass hills, where look! why, there! under the sun in the sky comes a pack of birds with bare heads and long curved necks, hanging in a fly above the most naked of bodies, that of John and Jill who sleep foot to head, head to foot, in the tall grass the cattle, these days and nights, lie around in. That is, the two or three of the herd left, counting the one on its back, quite uncowlike, with jowls stretched, legs spread, belly open to heat of sun.

The heat of the sun that warms the water in the horse bucket the Cattleman works his hands in, knifing coyote bone from leg meat, rib from gut. On the dirt comes moving shadow of birds flying overhead toward hills. The Cattleman sets down coyote rib on porch step and saddles up horse, whose blond chest and mane have flies going at what the sun has crusted of coyote blood. Cattleman unties horse reins, mounts horse, and out of saddlebag pulls pistol he loads with bullets strapped around his hips as horse moves up path grooved with horse-shoe chunks of dirt.

No one saw the Indian take the coyote rib off the porch step, break coyote rib over bent knee, take one bone of rib down to the low land where the Indian ties the cloth brown with blood of snake to bone of rib on the unbroken tip of the branch.

"See if I ever marry you again!" shouts Jill from up on the horse saddle, grabbing leaves off the trees the horse walks under, throwing leaves at the back of John's head. John leads the horse by reins along the stream rocks slow and steady now, as the Cattleman so says for him to do. The Cattleman sits behind Jill, Jill's dress around his neck, compass tied to saddlebag as he fires pistol up through the trees at nothing, it appears, up in the sky. And there is the horse. The horse stops to drink with the good load of not only the Cattleman and who seems to be the-always-naked Jill, only also there is the cow, cow tied by rope to saddle, pulled behind as horse drags cow on its back over rocks while frogs hop out of the waters onto the cow.

Down by the waters of the ocean, the Indian walks the black sand to where wood has drifted up along the sand banks. Wood black with tar. Here, the Indian sits in the sand, lays wood to tar to wood, lays tar to wood to tar.

"Put it on yourself!" shouts Jill, Jill now standing on porch step, holding horsehide dress the Cattleman has held the pistol to Jill's head to put this dress on if Jill wants to get to eat the cow John is dragging by rope to pit of rocks.

"Jillie Bug," says John, kicking cow head into pit, "if you love me, do as the man here says."

"Till death do you part," says the Cattleman, dropping dress into horse bucket.

Now comes the tying of cow feet, two in front, two in back, to rail of fence wood that rests on four legs of wood crossed and wedged by rocks into dirt around pit. Cow, on deader side of life, hangs by feet above the dry sticks the Cattleman sets to fire, who then with pistol, points John and Jill into cabin.

"Carry on," says the Cattleman, and the Cattleman hitches the door shut.

Once inside the cabin, this John, he runs to the cot, lies his back down, says "Hey, Jill, so what do you think?"

Jill picks up coyote leg with paw, takes smell of the matted fur, throws paw over at face of John, John lying there.

"Jill, Jill, Jill," says John, "take a look around, give it some thought now, lace curtains, some throw-rugs here and there, and this stove, what a stove, a stove like this we could cook ourselves up some fine hearty meals on!"

"Get this off me," says Jill, bending down.

So John undoes back of horsehide dress with horsehair tassels around the neck, and Jill, in her naked usual self, slides into arms of John onto the cot. These two, what honeymooners they are! as cot bends, cracks, breaks and John and Jill fall with bird feather floating up, and look what luck, there! right there lies pistol.

"What's all the ruckus?" shouts the Cattleman, who un-hitches the cabin door and opens cabin door wide in close range for this John, who aims pistol over Jill's naked shoulder, and who fires. Hits. Blood of Cattleman on cabin door, on porchboards and on down porch steps to where horse stands, lifts its head, hooves the dirt.

"My hero!" says Jill. "Let's eat!"

No one saw the Indian take the dress out of the horse bucket, take the compass off the saddlebag, take the dress and the compass down to the branch, wind the dress along the branch under coyote bone tied to cloth brown with blood of snake, hook the compass chain around the dress buttons. No one saw the Indian lift the deck of wood and tar and wood, carry deck on head across black sand to water, where Indian sets down deck, sits on knees on deck, stroking water with hands, going up over waves, then gliding out onto the farther waters of ocean.

THE GENERALS

My husband plays football.
Maybe you've heard of him.
His name is Ted Lawson.
There's a Ted Lawson who
plays in the Pros. That's not
him. My husband's Ama-
teur, first-string though—a
quarterback. Sure, he tried
out for the Pros, my hus-

band Ted did, hasn't everyone? He got drafted, traded, injured, put on waivers, and then was cut. That's how come I say maybe you've heard of him. My husband was a popular statistic in the press once.

He was the one whose shin bone popped through his calf. In photographs it looks as if his leg has acquired a second knee, this one lower, rested best on the turf. I couldn't see it when it happened. My seat was bad. Too high up. It was also on the side where fans were singing the carry-him-off-on-a-stretcher song. Carry him off was right. On the way to Sinai, he kept on asking what the score was, what quarter was it, what time-out were we on, where's the T.V., and where's Sinai, my husband wanted to know, why go there anyhow, Israel, Sadat, or Peru?

As I said, it was in all the papers.

My husband saved those press clips, framed them in maple, and hung them along the walls in our bedroom. A frame-by-frame instant replay with arrows pointing to the leg, before and after, the empty helmet, the fumbled football circled. This is to someday show to our kids, my husband assures me. We do not have any kids. Not any yet. But there's a lot running around the stadium across the street from where we live.

My husband's in training now. He trains with the kids in the street. They run pass-plays, dodge oncoming cars. Ted throws long bombs that bounce off windshields into kids' hands. These kids are professional. You should see how they can spike that ball, jump, do their dance. I watch from the sidewalk or what has been formally zoned the sidelines. The speed limit's thirty so cars must be going forty or more, sometimes swerving over the curb to avoid a broken pass-pattern, other times simply pressing the gas and waving the finger. Being the wife that I am, I yell at Ted, yelling for him to go find somewhere else to train. Find a parking lot, a battlefield—the stadium, why not use it? There's one kid who will always respond to this. This is the kid who prefers you to address him as Sir Gyro, the Gyronaut. He'll come striding over, slap me five, toss the ball from behind his back, say, "Ah, Ms. Ted, come on, you throw us a pass."

So, okay, all right, I try. Put my fingertips along the laces how my husband taught me. The ball goes wobbly. Hits the speed-limit sign. I don't know how my husband does it. He says all it is is knowing how to pass under pressure, that a four-wheel drive is a six-foot-six two-eighty-five-pound tackle, that all you have to do is keep your cool, or as Sir Gyro says, "You got to be far more so than cool, Ms. Ted, you got to be *ice*."

The other obvious part to being a quarterback is having an arm to do it with. My husband's arm, for example, is longer than the other. Last time we measured it was three and a fourth inches longer. He can shake his shoulder out of his back and gain a quarter of an inch in the process. From what I've seen, the arm grows about a half an inch per season. I found a shop to take his shirts to where they will alter sleeves at the cost of a hot dog, program, and beer. This is probably something only a woman would look for—the distance between the cuff and the wrist. Still, I think details like that can be significant when you are trying to sell life insurance part-time as my husband Ted is trying to do. "War bonds," he calls them, and before the start of this season, says he will have every Gladiator—that's his team, the Gladiators—sold, signed, and covered for life. No easy task is right. After a part-time day Ted returns, two kids under one arm, Sir Gyro under the other, calling, "Hey, lover, look! Steaks for dinner!"

The house is transformed.

The couch becomes the goal line.

The stairs, the goal.

They block, tackle, and dive. It is Ted's aim to get his body over the couch and up the stairs so he can change his shirt, go out and throw a few before dinner is served. Frozen hot dogs and warm beer. We eat all together in the light of the T.V. By the time dinner's done with, Ted will be asleep. You can know when he's asleep by how his arm hangs. It hangs off the corner of the couch into his plate. When he is awake it will not reach this far. It will reach to about the top of his can of beer.

Last night though, my husband Ted did not fall asleep. There we were, watching the latest sports coverage on the nature of football in Japan, and I felt Ted's hand come behind my neck, flop with my hair. Ted looked to the kids, to me, to the kids, the backs of their heads sprung up in front of the T.V.

"Hey, Gyro!" Ted called.

He has only to speak and each one will turn and look. I saw them looking at Ted, and you could know what would be coming next. Ted crawled off the couch, shook his shoulder out, let his arm drop, and screamed a peculiar scream for a man of his quality and size.

"Don't do that shit!" Gyro shrieked, and went running out, kicking the others along with him as he did.

"That kid's going to be a star someday," Ted said. "It's funny," he said, lifting my dress, "how you can tell already who is and who isn't."

My husband and I have been with each other since high school. That was when we first did. At least with each other, that is. It was under the bleachers as everyone else before us had done, leaving initials engraved in stilts, recording forever the boredom of lust. Ted's father was the football coach there, and this was during team practice—when else?—us camouflaged with cups of trash, faded programs, and runaway pompom strings while Ted's father drilled the team up the stairs and down the seats. A player's leg came falling through, and I heard Ted's father yell, "You, get up! Get off your butt!" and I got scared. Ted tried to cover me, ramming my forehead with his elbow which remains to be a part of him we never know what to do with in our hours of sleep.

After that one though, I had a headache that took me through History, with Ted sitting behind me, passing me notes that I still have. I know now that these were merely diagrams of defense and offense, Xs and Os drawn everywhere, kisses and hugs was what I was of course thinking of then. There are some I have where I'd written him back equally illogical facts, about Christians versus Lions, how the Coliseum of the Trojans, Olympics, and Rams was built after the one in Rome, how Vergil had torn his Achilles in P.E. class, and how it was Augustus who declared August the month of war.

This continued on through World War II.

By the time we'd advanced to Biology III, The Human, I was in the mind of predicting I was pregnant on a bimonthly basis. I think that was what had convinced Ted to convince himself to convince me to run away with him after the last game of the season. That and the fact that I have five brothers myself, them still in various degrees of high school learning, wrestlers who have led the state, year in and year out. Each at one time or another had challenged Ted to a match on our lawn, the youngest of my brothers taking Ted on when he was in his father's tux before the Senior Prom. Also, Ted's father had arranged for Ted the choice of two alternatives, to either attend his father's West Point alma mater, or to go study the true origins of the sport in Dublin at the Gaelic Academy of Rugby, neither of which seemed to Ted to be desirable outlooks for his future.

Last night, the future was now.

I kept on hearing Ted's father yell, and maybe this was because of the beer, thinking Ted's father was coming in via satellite through the T.V., yelling, "Lift those legs! Pick up your feet! This is not Home Economics! This is Life! Life! Life!"

That it is.

Ted does not speak of his father half as much as he used to. Before the fatal bypass, Ted's father was quoted in papers for saying, "Well, the boy never did learn how to scramble." That one is framed in mahogany. It hangs deadeye center in the lineup going across our wall. Maybe if Ted does con some Gladiators, we'll have a steady flow coming in so we can frame a few of these notes I have. I think it would be a nice addition to add to our collection, or what Sir Gyro calls, and I believe he got this from Ted, calling it our homemade wall of fame.

I read in Sports the other day that Ted Lawson, the Pro, got elected into the Hall of Fame. We met him once, Ted Lawson, my husband and I did. So did Sir Gyro. This was after my husband had returned from Sinai, arriving home on crutches to a bag filled with cards and letters sent from players and fans across the country and beyond. There was one that was a box. It was sent from Canada and its postage was due. I forfeited a trip to the sleeve shop to pay for it, thinking it might be an invitation for Ted to play Canadian league. I was wrong. It was chocolate broken and melted in parts of the cardboard box it came in, but you could see that at one point in its airmail career this chocolate was molded in the shape of a lifesize football. It was as big as that and the last remains of it are the laces which should carry me through another season of making brownies to give to Gladiators after home-team defeats. But out of all these greetings of sympathy, Ted Lawson's seemed to me the most heartening. Lawson had sent a typed letter and with it a picture his kid had drawn in crayon. It had a goal post missing a bar so it looked like a cross, the football looked like a lemon colored in yellow, and there was a player with six fingers on each hand, and one leg that, as it was, was shorter than the other. My husband magnetized the picture and the letter to our refrigerator door.

I will read from it now.

My son, Ted Jr., sends his regards and ditto do I. I hope your insurance can rake those front-office SOBs for more than you deserve. I agree, astro turf should be outlawed. It's pure cement. Gives you shinsplints in your head. My wife's a nurse and according to her, you should be dead by now if not on the road to sudden death. But look at you, out of surgery in a snap and walking so soon! I'd like to meet you, shake your hand, you know, will the real Ted Lawson please stand up?

How about coming to summer camp? It's outside
of Philly, nowhere really, but what else is there to do?
It's how the coach likes it—NO DISTRACTIONS—
another Adolf on the rise. But why am I telling you
this? Your old man's a coach, correct? So bring him,
your wife, your kids if you want, hell, bring the world!
Just make sure you bring yourself.

The trainer said he'd like to have a look at you.
You can get in a free massage, whirlpool, wax job, the
works.

So chin up, Lawson, we're rooting for you!

All the best,

Ted

(And his phone number which I won't list here. Let the
press try and find it for themselves.)

And so we went. That was three summers ago. Ted's
father could not come. He was going through explora-
tional physicals at the time, and told Ted that Ted had a moral responsibility to go there, to the camp, as a representa-
tive of both him and his father, the coach. But we did bring
Sir Gyro along. What choice did we have? We didn't have
the cash, and Sir Gyro's sister Slam was the top drug
dealer at the stadium then and had offered to pay for our
flights round-trip so long as we agreed to adopt Gyro on
weekends, which for her ran Monday through Friday. This
wasn't an up-front offer. It was found in an envelope under
our back door, written in Spanish which Gyro had to translate
for us, substituting Sir Gyro for Juan Carlos, I'm sure. Gyro
did not have to translate for us the signed blank check.
That we took directly to the airline counter that afternoon, got

on an airplane that evening, and flew off for Philadelphia that night.

Champagne in first class.

Two days later we arrived at camp. This is skimming past parts when Ted got his crutch caught in the airport's revolving door and, when getting onto one of those tricky moving walkways, fell where some fan apparently recognized Ted and asked for his autograph. This also skips over takeoff when Gyro slungshot a champagne cork at the steward, shouting, "What's so funny, you fag?" after Ted had made a joke about how this plane was the same kind of plane that soccer team crashed in on takeoff. Ted's humor seemed to give Gyro the humorous impulse to blow into the plug of your headset every time you thought you were finally asleep, and Ted had his turned on to a volume that, with mine on, I could clearly hear what Jimmy the Greek had been predicting as to who would come out fighting, who would fall away forgotten, and who would forge on ahead to the Super Bowl held in our own Memorial Coliseum that year.

Besides the lost baggage, which was supposedly delivered to our doorstep, there was the memorable fact that I forgot to bring Ted Lawson's letter along that had, of course, the crucial phone number listed in it. And so there was a night spent in the airport of Philadelphia, trying to place long-distance collect calls to Slam's phone machine, a maneuver which everyone knows an operator will not accept regardless of how many lies you tell, including trying to tell the truth of our story to one operator who laughed and then connected us with an international operator who Ted talked on with for hours about screen-pass options, the nickel defense, and quarterbacks in shotgun.

We never did reach Slam, or Slamantha the Slime as Gyro calls her, but we did reach her weekend boyfriend who also spoke Spanish but from a Cuban standpoint which Gyro said was lame to understand. We had to have Gyro ask him to break into our house, which is no major problem, though this boy-friend obviously did have a problem, breaking the back-door window and the back-door lock when we had firmly told Gyro to tell him where the hidden key was in the padding of the helmet on our doorstep. And then we had to pay Gyro an extra weekend's allowance for this United Nations transaction when the boyfriend finally called back the next day, with Ted Law-son's phone number, which the boyfriend recited to me direct from our kitchen phone, informing me that we were out of beer, that our hot dogs were moldy, and that we had a good breeze coming in through our back-door window, all reported in what else but perfect common English.

Sure, we tried asking people at the airport if they knew where the Generals' camp was but people would answer us, "The Generals? Who cares? They suck!" or "The Generals? You mean you want to get to Gettysburg?" And then of course Ted calling the number and having someone else answer and say, "No, he's in a meeting," or "No, he's in vespers," or "No, he's in practice," or "No, I don't know where he is," when all we wanted to know was where the camp was located. But that was highly confidential information we were told. How could they be sure we weren't rival spies? We'd have to call back, speak to the man himself.

We must have spent more making those calls than Slam did flying us round-trip first class because you had to have known the check was not hers. Maybe the time it took Slam to write the check and the adoption contract delayed her a payment from a client or two but these clients are patients, diehards as Gyro calls them, who will sleep at your doorstep if you promise them a delivery by sunrise.

My husband and I, in case you are wondering, do not partake in drugs. At least not anymore. In Amateur, you do not receive the benefits of free unlimited prescriptions as you are entitled to receive in the Pros.

However long it took, we did eventually get there. To the camp, that is. Ted Lawson was right. It was nowhere. I couldn't direct you there if you drove me yourself. It's so lost in trees and roads of wilderness that I was positive we'd entered into another continent and were traveling toward the center of it, if not toward the outskirts of its vague geographics. That makes no sense whatsoever, I know, but it's what I told my husband Ted, and Ted agreed. He said it was as if Watts were the Sequoias and the Sequoias were Siberia.

I think the jet lag was having its relative effects.

We had a rental car and Gyro drove, following Lawson's directions that stopped us at a gate. That's what it was, a gate. Chain-closed and on a fence that had a tarp over the other side so you could not see in. Up above the Generals' flag hung in no wind, and forward ahead a cop stood standing at the gate. He had a club, gun, and walkie-talkie mounted on his hips. We rolled down our windows and the heat eased in.

"What did we want?" the cop wanted to know.

"Did we have a pass?"

"An I.D.?"

"Ted Lawson?" the cop replied. "Right, and I'm Knute Rockne, nice to meet you, and who's this here? Joe Namath's mother? And I suppose you're O. J. Simpson?" The cop reached in and patted Gyro's head.

Gyro opened the car door into the cop's groin, and shouted how his sister Slam was a crack banker in Watts who would beat his pig ass up if he didn't let us in.

The cop adjusted his gun, and Gyro said, "Cool," got back into the car, shut the door, rolled his window up, and turned the A.C. on blast.

Ted was next. He got out of the car and limped his cast over to the cop. I watched Ted talk to the cop and point at us in the car and I waved. The cop did not wave back. He lowered his sunglasses, looked at Ted. Ted had his cast lifted and was showing with his hands how the leg broke at the shin. No, the cop shook his head, no. Ted limped back to the car, put his head through my window, and told us that practice was on, we'd have to wait for it to end, that we could sit here in the car until then, listen to the radio.

"You guys are royal drags," Gyro had to remind us.

Gyro pushed the driver's control button, and every window in the car went up. He turned the radio on, turned the speakers to stereo, and scanned the dial through crosswaves of opera and marching-band static.

I looked around for Ted and saw him sitting in the grass, the back of his head leaned against the fence. I took out my nail file and got out of the car. Outside, the air was difficult. It was not made for human purposes, I thought. Sure, you live next door to an eight-lane freeway, across the street from a stadium parking lot, and you will get your share of prime-stage smog alerts. But this air did not alert you. It slept on you. Mild as a Darvon. I sat down next to Ted and the level of oxygen seemed to lower in my head. It was takeoff again. I said this to Ted.

I said, "Where's the oxygen mask?"

"Did you hear that?" Ted asked.

I saw he had his eyes closed.

"Listen," he said.

Claps. Calls. A whistle. Helmets hitting helmets.

"That was a seventy-three-score X up and out," Ted explained.

He looked to me and took my nail file. I watched him slipping it between his skin and the cotton coming out of the cast. The cast reached above his thigh. He scratched.

"My dad developed that," Ted said. "That and the sixty-two-score to the tight end."

We sat there for more than a couple of hours it seemed to me. I had done my fingernails and toenails and fingernails and was ready to begin on the toes of Ted's cast when it must have been a football that hit from the other side, shaking the fence we were leaning on.

"Failed Omaha," he said, my husband, seeming to smile.

My husband's smile can be hard to decipher. His teeth have this natural gray tint and that team dentist could not find the caps to match. I can often be distracted by this and will have to look again to see what my husband may possibly be feeling now, or showing to feel, with that mouth of his.

The lights around the fence, I hadn't noticed them until they came on. When they did it became as bright as any stadium you've ever been in. They made the grass look greener and the heat seem hotter. How much longer could they, the Generals, go on like this in this lack of air? This was nothing, Ted said. He said evening practice was easier than morning when you'd have to wake up at five for vespers, six for breakfast, and seven for practice that lasted past noon in full pads.

Full pads—that's neck pads, shoulder pads, elbow pads, rib pads, hip pads, thigh pads, knee pads, et cetera pads.

"You can hear that, can't you?" Ted asked. "They're not playing in full pads now."

By the time the gate opened, the cop had gone and Gyro had ODed asleep on static and A.C. Ted helped me stand and I stood by the opened gate, watching. It was as if you were there watching them descend from the locker-room tunnel after a defeat, their heads down, their steps slow from hip to foot. But this was after a practice, a game of Us versus Us, so to speak, and I had never seen anything like it: some, with helmets on, had mud dried on face bars, chin straps torn off, mouth guards spit out, others were peeling helmets off, bending ear lobes, the flat-topped heads, and Afros pressed in sculpted reliefs, canals of the brain, I thought, these inner helmet pads, and necks large as arms, arms large as thighs, thighs the width of twice a thigh, ripped jerseys rolled high above chests, the breathing ribs, and the yank of the string on shorts, shorts undone to the jock, blades of grass and blood on knees, shot-put calves, shaved calves, taped ankles, shoes untied, and cleats digging dirt. Not one saying a word. One after one. Each seeming slower and slower. I stood by watching and the few who saw me, a woman, these few turned their heads, their eyes down toward the ground they walked on. I felt I should not have been there, that this was not what a woman should see and not when a man should have to see a woman see him. After all my pleas of wanting to visit my husband that one summer he had with the Pros in camp, I realized then, being there and seeing this, that these were men who belonged with men.

A football hit me broadside in the head.

"Heads up!" I heard and I saw my husband waving, and Gyro standing next to him out on the field, along with a player who I knew had to be the man himself, Ted Lawson, the Pro.

Lawson jogged toward me. He picked up the ball, slapped it between his hands. He said his wife was sorry she couldn't make it. She was in her seventh month and not feeling too good, he said. He had a bleeding lip. The bottom one. It looked as though a tooth had gone through it. You could practically see the taste of it. Lawson walked me across the field. This was real turf raked in chunks of mud and grass, sod my foot got caught on and Lawson was there to catch me.

"You guys hungry?" Lawson asked. "There's an all-you-can-chow if you guys want."

"Fuck chow!" Gyro said. "Let's play ball."

Lawson rubbed his eyes with the back of his wristband. He had one eyebrow that went straight across. It must have been sweating into his eyes. He rubbed his eyes some more and tossed the ball to my husband. My husband looked to me slightly lopsided in his cast. But his hands, they were in balance, spinning the ball, catching it, spinning it, catching it.

"I'll kick both your ass!" Gyro said.

My husband looked to Lawson.

Lawson looked to my husband.

The players took their positions.

I took a seat on the sideline bench.

My husband was center, quarterback; Lawson to the side,

wide receiver; Gyro head on with Lawson, defensive corner-back. I could hear the calls. The two forty-eight, set, hut one, hut two, hike, hike.

Gyro and Lawson shot off.

I watched my husband. No six-foot-six two-eighty-five-pound tackle, and no four-wheel drive, the only pressure to keep his cool was the pressure of his own body, of the foot of the cast sinking in mud, the shoulder shaking out, the arm elbowing back, the free arm extending forward, pointing downfield toward the goal, aligning the body as to where the ball ought to go. It went. The ball went spiraling in an arc above; I don't know how these lights don't blind. I looked to my husband. He was standing there alone in the field, watching the ball, his pass, waiting to see, I thought, if he was great, average, or bad, if, as the saying goes, that behind every great receiver there stands a great quarterback.

Lawson was sprinting, arms pumping, yards beyond Gyro who had stopped, it appeared, to witness a Pro in the act. The ball was approaching Lawson, coming over from behind his head—the timing—his head at the last moment turning to look, the arms outstretched, legs straightening out from under him, biology of the human body defined, linear, lengthwise through the air into a diving fingertip catch over the goal line, a somersault roll, and quick up to the feet, the prance, the arms lifted above the head, the shouts of Lawson-to-Lawson! Touchdown! Score!

The fans go wild!

The bench is cleared!

Delirium spreads!

We won! We won! We won!

"Did we win?" my husband asked. "Tell me again," he asked, "did we win or did we lose?"

This was last night in bed. The question an often one, be it pre-, post-, or during the season, the question is always an often one asked. From across the street the stadium, the Coliseum, its torch burned a light that entered in through our bedroom window. My husband's face, I could see it there, eyes closed, and waiting. The elbow at my forehead, the arm held behind his head, and the leg, I could feel it looking for a place for itself, the metal brace cool in its touch to the skin.

"Did you hear me?" my husband asked. "I asked you a question," he said. "Did we win or did we lose?"

What does your husband ask you at night in bed?

And what, if I may ask, do you say to your husband?

Do you say to your husband, for example, in one way or another, whatever your case may be, something on the order of, No, dear, there wasn't a game, you're in training now, remember? Or do you choose, if you choose to say anything at all to your husband, could you choose to say something to the effect of, Yes, dear, Oh, yes, you won, they carried you off the field, remember? The players, the press, the fans, the kids, the coaches, everyone carrying you up on their shoulders high, and you there, upholding above you your heart for your father, a Pro, a true Pro you were, like Aeneas you were, Aeneas, indeed.

LET ME HAVE

you

"Hey!" shouts my brother. "Hey, out here in the desert you get hurricanes, hurricanes of sand that shoot at your face. Say, driving, like this, with this *this* windshield, what do you do? You stick your head out, that's what you do, stick your head out the window, like this, or better, even better more, you get these goggles, hang-gliding goggles with a mask, a nylon mask that covers everything of all of your face, put those on and put this, your head, out the window, like this, to steer—and we'll go do that, *okay?*—We'll go out hang-gliding off those mountains over there, that's where we'll go, and this rock, there's this one rock that looks just like me, me, your hero, me! It's great, you fly right off my head, it's really great! And climbing, climbing in hurricanes, what you do is you go out always, *always* in your shorts, shorts like these right here—no shoes, no shirt, no mask—and hey, look at my face, what a face, face of a hero or what? It's great, it's really great, I really love it here! Isn't it great?"

"Look, hey," my brother shouts, "I've got friends, all these desert friends you'll have to meet, too so many friends to fit on the boat! My boat? Sure it's big! Of course mine's big! You think I'd have one, *mine*, that wasn't big? Me, I'm booked up from now until whenever, booked up ten friends a ride, ten days a week, rise at three a.m., drive boat to lake, put friends on boat, water ski, no skis. Wet suit? Who needs it? Snow? Blizzard, make it a blizzard, and hey, so my teeth, you see these teeth? Go ski your teeth on ice, that's what you get, you get what you want—*friends*. The friends, they say, Tom, Tommy, we love you, and then they all place bets on when I'm going to die. It's great, every day I'm alive they owe me ten cents each! I'll be a trillionaire before I reach forty, used to think fifty, now, now I think forty. What do you think? Think you can ski ice on bare feet? I know you know I can and you want to know why I know you know? I'll tell you why, it's because, you know, I never, *never* get sick! Made up shirts, I NEVER GET SICK on the back, KCIS TEG REVEN I on the front for all the friends following like rearview sirens behind. All my friends, they all wear my shirts, day and night, night and day! Hey, look, there goes one now! I ask you, is this great or is this great?"

"Hey, okay, so, hey!" shouts my brother. "You see this house? I bought this house, *me*. This house is mine, mine, mine! Me and the girls—you'll meet the girls—the girls, they call this Tommy's house-in-the-desert-fun, and fun we have! Bras in the dishwasher, garters on the stove, nylons in the freezer—what more do you want? What more do you want me to say? Say, head-in-the-oven? Okay, head-in-the-oven, *there*, I said it. Get a wife, a wife of your own. I owned a wife, a wife I raked ten cents a day with, a wife I lost a losing bet to, to come home and call, Hey, where are you? Hey, where'd you go to? Look, you see this phone? This is the greatest phone that ever lived. You turn it on, like this, push this button here and it dials itself by itself, dials the ski lodge, you, in your trillionaire days, will own, and here, look, hear the voice of her who answers? What's she say? She says, Hello, can I help you, hello? I love her. I love that girl. I put her on this, my answer machine. It's great, the girls call up, they hear her tape, they go, Tom, Tommy, is that *you?*"

"So, well, okay, okay," my brother shouts, "I eat breakfast at dinner, dinner at lunch, lunch I skip. Hey, you see a gut on this guy? That's right, you don't. What you see, you see, is out here in the desert you can go, say, three hours of sleep, say, every three or so days so you get all this extra time to count and sit and count how many pans and pots and saucers and cups and plates and bowls and spoons and forks and knives you have that you don't really all that much anymore need. And then you figure for every pan, pot, saucer, cup, plate, bowl, spoon, fork, knife, how much you can sell each one for to all your friends that really—it *really* is amazing how easy it is to make friends here—and then, then you get them, your friends, to raise you five to twelve cents a day, and everyone agrees on ten so long as you do this skydive out of a burning F-fourteen, and that's all great, you yank the cord before you see your head in the rock, and hey, so, so what's a back for, anyhow? And then what you do is is you quit your job you're fired from. Say, hey, it's my birthday, I quit! Make a new job, make *you* your boss, go boss to executive, executive to president, president to chief, chief to king, with ten cents a day, ten-twenty a shirt pouring in day after day after day, and bumper stickers! You start thinking, bumper stickers, NO U-TURN ON THE ROAD TO FUN—sold out of those, did you want one of those? I can get you one, I really can, I can, I can, you know I can, if anyone can it's *me*, your brother, *me!*"

"This way, this way!" shouts my brother. "Over here! What do you do with all these? All these dresses, dresses, dresses? You rip off the arms, that's what you do! Rip off the arms, like this, tie them shoulder to wrist, wrist to elbow, and there, you've got yourself a flying scarf—sharp or what? And then you get a knife, a knife like this right here, and cut them, these, the silk ones up knees to arms, arms to knees, you see, and needles! Get a needle, get a thread, thread the needle, and sew, sew, sew, sew, sew the silks up, like this, and then, then what you do is take this broomstick and take this mop and put them end to end together, see? Drop some of this nail polish in, like this—forget the glue, use this, this polish stuff really, really, really sticks—and then you needle and thread, thread and needle, the silks to the broomstick and mop, like this! And hey, rip off that mop head—that, that you can just throw out—who needs it? I don't need it. Do *you* need it?

"And belts! Belts, belts, belts, what do you do with all these belts?! You belt them together, that's what you do, belt them buckle to strap, strap to buckle into two big belts, like these, like this, you belt them around this broomstick and mop, like this, and then you take them, these belts like this, between your legs, and up, you see, like this, over your gut, your chest, and up your shoulders, like this—Boy, did the wife *love* belts or what?—and then, you cross them under your shoulders, like this, down your back and up again between your legs, and then you buckle, buckle, buckle, buckle yourself up tight and raring-ready to go!—and, hey, wait, hey, what's going on up there? Can you see? Am I caught? Is that that light bulb hanging down there again?—Okay, all right, okay, so you see what I mean, you see.

"So what do you say? You want a dress? Take a dress! Take a skirt! How about a blouse? You like this blouse? I like this blouse! This, the wife's favorite blouse! Here, try it on, go ahead, oh, come on, go ahead, try it on, *it's not going to kill you!* Okay, okay, okay, so how about a brush? Want a brush? Here, have a brush, take this one, no, here, let me, there, how's that? Feels great or what? And hair! Hair, hair, hair, all this hair, add it all up, twenty cents a hair! Hair in the sink, hair in the carpet, hair in the blanket, hair in the couch, hair in the oven, add it all up, sell it all off, who knows, maybe someone will make a wig somewhere and maybe someone will maybe think, was that from the sink or from the carpet or from the blanket or from the couch or from the oven or from the me, the Tom, the me?

"And sunglasses! Sunglasses, you got to have sunglasses! So what you do, you see, is take ones like these, and then you take these nylons—please, I wish you'd take some of these nylons, *please*—and cut holes, two holes to each thigh, like this, slip it over your head, like this, make room for the glasses, and hey! What do you got?! You got your flying mask, that's what! And I ask you, am I, your brother, me, a genius or what?"

"Come around this way," my brother shouts, "over this way here! See that ledge? That's my knee. Put your foot right there—look out for my hip! No! Not there! Does that look like a hip? Okay, okay, there you go, now come on, hurry, the winds, they're dying, hurry! Here, grab my chin, *that*, that right there, here, let me have you, give me your hand, let go and give me your hand—look this way, not *that* way—okay, up, up, up you go! There, now, wasn't that great? Okay, now what you do is you move over here, have a seat. There's tons of room, *believe me*—I should know—I had girls and friends and girls up here all at once for the wife's throwing-away party, and hey, whose head is it anyway? Now look, look, see how the wind blows the dust off my hip? Okay, so what you got to do, what that means is you got to go off from this side over here. Look out, hey, sorry, okay, now, okay, okay, now you start like this.

"Belts fastened? Check!

"Mask strapped? Check!

"Silks tied? Check!

"Mop-broom? Check!

"Scarf on? Check!

"Shoes off? Check!

"Kiss your sister? Check! Check!

"Okay, you ready? I'm ready! You ready? Okay, let's take it on three—ONE, TWO—hey, where's your spirit? Get some spirit! Come on, hey, count along! Here we go, we go—ONE, TWO, THREE!"

FLAG OF HAWAII

This is for the Captain, *ke Kapena*, may your heart rest in peace. Nw no longer the bachelor, I can see you there on the altar, standing upon some ship, looking over water, your Pacific, Oahu, a honeymoon awaits you beyond. May yours be simple, outdoors where God will overlook you, or look down upon you, or so as you may remember this is what we at one time appeared to have had agreed. The Father, the Son, the Holy Ghost, they are here with me. We salute you. Half-mast waves the flag of Hawaii.

Ahoy! Today is a day of mourning, a day to mourn a memory, the memorial of you, Captain, yours, of how I first saw you, you with your medallions of some Adonis, an explorer who knew what he had come for. You, Captain, you knew what you had come here for. You came, you saw, you anchored my harbor, my God. The Virgin Mary witnessed this. May she be the virgin to christen your ship. Break a bottle on the bow, the stern, the altar. The bells of the buoys are ringing now.

This gift you gave, Captain, this that you called your bible, an atlas, what you wrote to me within remains. You say here how you love, dear, lovely, how you wish, want, yearn, how there is time and space, eternal. Here you, you Captain yourself, you say for me to please enjoy this gift of your love forever. How long is forever for? Speak now or forever yearn for peace.

Captain, you spoke of your women as islands, every one of your women, an island, Hawaiian, divine. Your nights on Kauai and your wreck in Kahoolawe, your loss of Molokai and her sister Lanai, your longings for Maui and your hell with Hawaii, Oahu and you in her Honolulu. These your women, Captain, they are drifting, they are drowning, they are falling overboard. Cast down the lifevests, the lifeboats, the oars. Your women are calling you, Captain. Calling you, mayday! Calling you, S.O.S.!

. . .

He who fell before you, the late Captain James Cook, he was a captain who followed the path of Venus around and around the world. Here in the world of Hawaii, your natives took him to be their God but, in the end, your same natives took his life. Death by a dagger, this captain lie face down in the waters he himself claimed to have had discovered. Mercy falls upon you, Captain, no more tours around the world, no more greetings as God, no more harbors there to welcome you. Bless your blessed anchor, bless it now before you, Captain, for once it is lost, Captain, no one, not even yourself, can be saved.

Here, then, is where I leave you, Captain, as you yourself once left me. May your bride be the discovery, the island, to you who I never was. May you glorify her, your bride, sacred as the harbor, Pearl. May you comfort her through war and through peace, in victory and in defeat, past death to forever, if ever, never part. The Father, the Son, the Holy Ghost, we all of us here bow our heads for this moment of silence, a moment of prayer, an Amen, Amen.

Hoist the flag!
Anchors aweigh!
May God be with you on your ship.

DINNER

One night, when the family was sitting together at the table for dinner, the father said, "You know, I think it'd be nice if someone said a little Grace here for a change."

The father looked a-round the table for volunteers.

There were his three sons, and their mother, his wife. The eldest son sat at one head of the table, picking his teeth with a knife, and the middle son sat next to the father, tilting back on the legs of his chair, and the youngest son sat directly opposite facing the father, drinking a glass of milk, and as for the mother, she sat at the other head of the table, folding a dish towel end to end.

"Or is Grace a little too goddamn much to ask for?" the father said.

The eldest son put down his knife.

"I said it last time," he said.

"Bull, you did," the middle son said.

"You're all bull," the youngest son said. "I always say it."

"*Grace*," the mother said. "*There!*"

"You know," the father said, "when I was a kid, we'd be lucky if we even had this on our table." The father picked up a bottle of milk for all to see and then he slammed it down on the table. The milk in the glasses shook.

"Well," the middle son said, "when I was a kid, I had a father who'd make us say Grace every night for dinner."

The youngest son laughed.

"You think that's funny, don't you?" the father said. "I bet you all think that's funny, don't you? Well, one of these days you're all going to see just how goddamn funny it is to try to put some goddamn food on some goddamn table."

"*Amen*," the mother said. And then she looked up, and said to the father, "Can I serve now?"

"Sure!" the father said. "Who's stopping you?" And he threw his arms up and his elbow came down and hit the middle son next to him in the head.

"God, Dad," the middle son said, "I'm sure." The middle son rubbed his head with his hand and then looked at his hand.

"Don't you 'God, Dad' me," the father said, and he took a drink from his glass of milk, and put the glass down on the table, and said, "You know what your problem is? I'll tell you what your problem is. Your problem is your head's always in the way, that's your problem. Your head's too big!"

"Oh, boy," the mother said, and she got up from the table and took the folded dish towel with her and went to the kitchen counter where a roast beef was waiting on a platter. The mother took out a long knife and held the folded dish towel on the side of the platter and began cutting the strings off from around the roast beef. The rest of the family sat there with their plates before them watching the mother. The father sat with his arms crossed.

"Who wants the strings?" the mother called, and the youngest son raised his hand and jumped up from his chair.

"Why does *he* always get the strings?" the eldest son asked.

"Because he has growing blood," the mother explained.

The father and his sons watched the youngest son take the strings from the mother and put them in his mouth and suck on them and pull them, one by one, slowly out of his mouth and then put them back on the platter where the roast beef was. Then the youngest son went back to his chair at the table and sat down.

"Wipe your mouth," the father said.

"I did," the youngest son said, and he lifted his arm up and wiped his sleeve across his mouth.

"Is that the way you wipe your mouth?" the father said.

"I want more than anyone!" the eldest son yelled. "I want more than anyone else in the world!"

"Quit rocking your chair," the father said to the middle son. "You're going to wreck it. Do you know how much a chair like that costs?"

The middle son let the front legs of his chair drop back down on the kitchen floor and when he did, the arms of his chair hit the table hard enough to shake everything on it, including the stems of the flowers in the vase on the table.

"What planet are you on?" the father said.

The youngest son laughed, and the father said to the mother, "Did you see what your I.Q. son just did?"

The mother kept on slicing the roast beef. Some slices of beef lay side by side on the platter and some of the juice from the blood of the beef had gone off the side of the platter and onto the kitchen counter, and some had gone off the kitchen counter and onto the kitchen floor, and some had gone through the folds of the folded dish towel held in the mother's hand.

"Who wants the blood?" the mother called, and the youngest son sprung up from his chair and stood there waiting at the kitchen counter.

"He always gets to get everything!" the eldest son said.

"He's your brother," the father said.

"There's enough for everyone," the mother said.

The mother took out a large spoon and lifted the platter from one side and angled the platter toward her and spooned the spoon into the juice from the blood of the beef gathered along the rim of the platter. The youngest son opened his mouth and closed his eyes, and the mother spooned him some spoonfuls while the rest of her family sat there watching. Then the youngest son went back to his chair at the table and sat down.

"Good?" the father said.

"I guess," the youngest son said.

"I want mine rarer than raw!" the eldest son yelled. "I want mine barely dead!"

The mother put the spoon down on the strings on the side of the platter and she folded the folded dish towel over itself and picked up the long knife and resumed the slicing of the roast beef on the platter.

"You know," the mother said, "it's usually the man who does this."

"Someone get up and help your mother," the father said.

The youngest son stood up.

"Not you," the father said, and he turned to look to the middle son. "You," he said, "Mister I.Q., get up and help your mother."

"I don't need any help," the mother said.

"Nag, nag, nag," the father said, and he backed his chair into the kitchen counter to stand up.

"It's almost done now, sit down, it's fine, thank you," the mother said.

The father went to sit back down and when he did his elbow brushed against his glass of milk hard enough to knock the glass of milk over and milk spilled over the table and onto his chair and onto the lap of his pajamas.

"Christ Almighty," the father said.

"Christ Almighty," the middle son said.

"Look, pal," the father said, and he leaned into the middle son and the middle son leaned into the eldest son. "I don't need any backwash from you," the father said.

"Backwash?" the middle son said. "Backwash?"

The father stood up.

"Get up," the father said.

"Sit down," the mother said. "Come on, we're about to eat," she said, "sit down."

The mother had put the long knife aside and had come over with the folded dish towel and had begun toweling milk up off the table and off the chair and off the lap of the father's pajamas.

The eldest son stood up then and leaned over around the mother and the father and stole a slice of roast beef off the platter and began to eat it, and the youngest son yelled, "Hey, that's mine! Put it back!"

"I said," the father said, "get up!"

The father brushed the folded dish towel away and took hold of the collar of the shirt on the middle son's neck and tore some of the collar off the shirt in the process of lifting his son up to stand.

"Now," the father said, "let's hear you say that again."

The middle son rubbed the back of his neck, and said, "God, Dad, *God*."

"Okay, you two," the mother said. "That's enough," she said, "come on, sit down, let's eat, it's time to eat."

The father picked up his empty glass.

"Don't be silly," the mother said. "Give me that," she said, and she tried to take the empty glass from the father's hand.

The middle son sat down in his chair.

"I said," the father said, "get up!" and he pulled the middle son back up and the chair fell over backward onto the kitchen floor.

"Now look what you've done!" the father said. "That was a goddamn brand new chair!"

The mother bent down around the father's legs to try to

pick the chair back up and then the mother tried to towel milk up off the father's slippers and up off the kitchen floor, and the mother also tried to towel off the juice from the blood that had dripped down on the kitchen floor off the eldest son's stolen slice of roast beef.

The eldest son picked up his knife and banged the end of it on the table, and said, "Come on, let's go, I'm starving, let's eat!"

"Me, too!" the youngest son screamed, and he stood up on the seat of his chair. "Me, too!" he screamed. "I'm starving! Let's eat!"

The mother stood up then from bending down on the kitchen floor, and said to the father, "Your sons are starving."

The father raised the empty glass and pressed the rim of it up under the middle son's chin. "What's that look on your face for?" the father said. "I could break that look right off your face, you know that?" the father said.

The eldest son stepped over the fallen chair on the kitchen floor and pushed aside the middle son and now stood there taller than the father.

"You're in my way!" the father yelled. "Get out of my way!" the father yelled. And then looking around at all of them standing around him, the father raised the empty glass and holding it above him, above all else, the father yelled, "This means all of you! Every single goddamn one of you, out of my way!"

"Okay, okay," the mother said. "Grace is over," she said, and she took the empty glass from the father's hand and set it down on the table and eased the father back into his chair.

HER NAME IS WAHOO

It is mating season for the coyotes now. I find it pleasant to watch with binoculars from the porch in my backyard. I am not some kind of animal pervert. Nor are the coyotes ones. They watch, too. You can see how once the sniffs have been done, the forepaws raised, the bites to the neck exchanged, how fellow coyotes will all come gather around, drop whatever rabbit or bird they are chewing on, to get a front-row view of the lift of the tail, of the mount, and of the letting go when mates slowly lay themselves down on the ground. I have grown fond of that part, them slowly lying down. Often, when I am narrating to my dog, they will come to this part and I will not know what to call it. For a while, it was the victorious surrender part, but now I am not so sure if that is what it actually is of. Neither victory, nor surrender.

Events like these are not always so easy to get to watch. Sometimes a wind will come blow the backyard dirt around, and the time it takes to rub a handkerchief over the lens will most times lose you at least half, if not all, of the romantic conduct. Most times, though, it is my dog Wahoo who directs attention elsewhere, her clawing from the inside through the outside of the porch screen door, barking and howling and yelping like there's a coyote consuming her favorite raw-egg supper out of the pan on the porch. And once Wahoo has begun her vocal orchestrations, it is only moments between before you hear a neighbor's gun go off, and once that has occurred, you might as well wrap the binocular straps up, call it a day, go see which window—living, dining, or bed—has been shot through this time, because when coyotes around here hear the shot of a gun, be it a shotgun, handgun, rifle, BB, or otherwise, they do not stick around to observe the current human crisis. They are gone. Gone before you can even see if what they did was run, walk, or skip into the years of brush that lie beyond, sitting there on the porch in your backyard.

Of course this porch was not always here, and neither did

guns abound as they do now. When all us neighbors first moved here there were no porches, nothing but piles of dirt for a yard, and red flags tied to posts so you would know where your one-eighth-acre lot began and precisely where the end of it was. Some of the houses did not have windows put on, and there was the general experience everyone seemed to share in the complaints of, of electric garage doors that opened up on their own, and then never, not by taking a crowbar to it and running a rope to your truck, could you ever get those doors to quit their electric hum and come back down. The time I am thinking of was when the workers were still drilling for water, and then discovered a hot spring the size of a river that flooded us all, when this neighborhood of ours was called El Coyote, not El Camino Real, and when weekly meetings were planned to be held in whoever's turn it was backyard. That plan came through all right. There was one meeting back then, and it appears to hold the title of the first and last neighbors' meeting I have and will ever most likely be invited to attend.

It must have been birthing season for the coyotes then. They were probably looking for food to feed their pups. I think it no minor wonder then that that got them climbing in through windows, or the lack thereof, getting my dog Wahoo to run barking under a bed or under a couch. One or two of the neighbors had pet cats snatched, and once I spotted a coyote trotting down a sidewalk, a feline Siamese hanging from the coyote's mouth. Sometimes you would get them down in the basement, drinking up a reservoir of flood, but most times for me it was the garage. They would be there, panting in the shade of my truck, and I would stand, with one foot in the house, one in the garage, throwing whatever I could find in reach to throw, whole cartons of eggs and jars of lard I used to have stacked and stored, trying to hurry them out so I could get on going in my truck, not have to miss for the fifth or sixth time what would have been my first day of work at a new job, me then having the hope of becoming more than a hoser of pens at the pet kennel someday. And then there was that back-yard baby incident, when some coyote came into a backyard, took off with a newborn child, and all that was left was an emp-ty playpen to look into and a small configuration of blood on the playpen rug. It is an awful thought to think of, but often I do, of how coyotes are known to eat their prey alive.

But this now being the month of February, and not the birthing month of May, you get days when the desert rains come down, and you will not scope a coyote no matter how sincere your interests are. The air smells like a wet dog come in from the rain, and buckets of bugs pour themselves onto the porch screen door. From here on the porch, I can hear Wahoo sliding her paws across the linoleum floor, knocking over chairs and boxes, maybe a table or two, her nails sounding to me like they could use a bit of trimming some. Something about the loud of thunder seems to invite the dog to do this, like she is trying to dig a hole down through this house to the ground below, her having already dug through every inch of carpet the house has to offer, upstairs and down. I myself will often mistake these porch-shaking sounds for the shot of a neighbor's gun, and find myself ducked and crouched, look-ing out between the slats of my chair. Times such as this, there is nothing more to do but wonder when the rain will stop, if the dog will settle, and why it was I had to at that first and last neighbors' meeting suggest the plausible need for guns.

This meeting, it being held in the baby's mother's back-yard, with all us neighbors there sitting around a fire, I guess I felt it some sort of honor of mine to speak what I know of coyotes, having just been watching some tapes I had rented on Dogs and Men and Survival in General, thinking then I understood the fears these people have about the coyote, the prairie dog. For the coyote is wise. I told them that. I said, You cannot underestimate the wisdom of the coyote. And they are quick, too. Quicker than you can load, line it up, and shoot. Now if they're in your backyard, you can use a handgun, but once a coyote breaks beyond, say, the length between your door and the end of your yard, a handgun's a shaky shot. Once a coyote gets farther out, a shotgun could do you well, but coyotes don't do circles like the ones in your local amusement park. These coyotes, wild like they are, can dart in and out, diagonal like a jackrabbit does. And once a coyote's into the brush, you'll need a rifle, and then all you'll likely be doing is staring at horizons of mustard and brush, wondering just where that coyote was. You can tie meat to toy bombs but, chances are, you'll wreck your yard. And BBs will certainly scare them off, but the coyote's scare is a short-lived one. Your best bet, in all, is a wide range of guns, and all you've got to do is just shoot one of them, one coyote, and then leave it there for the rest of the pack to come up and smell, and that will get them all moving along. Coyotes may mate for life, I said, may be loyal to the pack, but not when there is death around.

So it only might figure that after such a sermon, a neighbor such as the one who had introduced himself as, "I'm the first house on the left," would now, when the weather is fine, be seen sitting out on his front porch, polishing an array of guns.

His real name is George but if I call him right out, "Hey, George!" like I did, him once passing me by with my truck fender hanging from the garage, he will say, "Mr. George Clancey Smith to you," so I just as well call him "the first house on the left" because that is just anyhow how I see him as. The first house on the left, with the shades pulled down, a white stationwagon car, and a barbwire sort of picket fence that borders in a crabgrass lawn. I sometimes think this man Smith is a direct descendent of Jed, Jedediah Strong Smith, though I have no legal proof on the matter, only that I think it was him, my neighbor Smith, that is, who shot my dog's eye out once—it has grown together fairly well now like a bite on the arm from a dog will, if you use electrical tape and seal it up tight as any good stitch-job would do. Further, it is how the man walks that makes me think he comes from the same blood as Jed Smith. This man has the walk of a tired man, a man whose knees do not properly serve him right, and I figure a fur trapper like Jed Smith, after having crossed the Great Salt Desert, west to east, Sierra Nevada, south to north, that a man of that distance would carry on to family that followed an implied fatigue of sorts.

Fatigued or not, it was the mother who was the one I kept on looking at that night. How fatiguing it must have been for her to have to get up from the dirt, where the rest of us were, to hang the rug over the rail of the playpen. Her doing this seemed to me to follow the howls of the coyotes you heard, and for some reason, the rug just kept on falling off. I do not know why. Maybe it was too heavy for the rail or maybe the mother was not setting it on the rail right. Either which way, it did. The rug would fall off, and the mother would then have to get up and dust it off and hang it back on the rail. This is when I wonder if I could have been more farsighted in my thoughts to think ahead instead of bringing my dog Wahoo along like I did, no leash or collar. Wahoo would have to get up, every time the mother did, to investigate the rug for herself, shaking her head, and making sounds with her nose like it was stuffed. Sometimes I think the dog has asthma. Maybe a little bronchitis, too. Wahoo also was not showing of herself a well-mannered dog, having taken a jump at a bag of potato chips Smith had brought, taking the bag and not eating one, just carrying it and dropping it next to me where she began to dig dirt up into the neighbors, and into the fire some, her not ever pausing to look or stop when I kept on telling her, "Wahoo! No! Sit! Heel! Stop!" And then I tried to take the bag away from her, and she let out some form of a growl, more like a gargle coming deep from the lungs, driven she was, to get that bag of chips buried, covered, and urinated on, which she did finally do, lifting her back leg up like your average male dog does.

It makes honest sense to me that someone would speak up on this, this being Smith to have spoken first, flicking his cigarette, and asking, "What's your dog? What kind of dog you got there? You sure that's a dog?" And the mother, she stood up saying how glad she was to have this brought up, that that dog does not look like a dog, that she did not know what that dog looked like but it for sure to her did not look like a dog. And Smith took a stand beside her, asking to them all, "Well, why don't we take a vote on it? Let's vote if the dog is a dog." And the mother agreed, saying how voting was really the only democratic thing to do. I recall having looked down at Wahoo then, and what was the dog doing but twisting herself on her back in the dirt, with some long drool going out of the side of her mouth that you did not need binoculars for to see.

Now I don't have the papers to prove it, and this is what I told them, told all those neighbors around the fire. I said, I don't have the papers to prove it. I got this dog off the road, and she may not be your most likely example of an encyclopedia dog, but who do you think would know that more than I do? Who do you think bathes her in cod oil to rid her of this scabby crud growing along her head? Who do you think feeds her lard every night to try to get her coat looking soft? Who do you think cuts these cyst-wads out, and who do you think gives her her monthly distemper shots, even though I have never once seen this dog—and her name, by the way, is Wahoo—and never have I seen Wahoo kill anything more than a house-trapped potato bug, and even then she was just playing with it, played until it rolled up into a tiny ball. And so I went on talking in that fashion until I was interrupted by my own dog when she let out a bark. A short, singular, sort of off-tune bark.

"What is it?" the mother asked.

"Tell her to sic it, why don't you," said Smith.

You could hear something going on in the brush back there. You could not see out past the light of the fire, but you knew what was out there. By day, it was land flat, dry and far as the mind is known to take you.

I got up and threw a log on the fire. This was not some heroic gesture of mine. I was hoping Wahoo might follow my lead, act like a dog, go running barking off into the dark, aimless. Wahoo did not move. She stayed there lying down, ears pointed back, forepaws crossed, letting out an occasional one-note bark. She put about as much effort into it as she does the milkman. Still Wahoo to me looked elegant in her pose. Crud, cysts and all, this dog had something regal about her, and I guess I was feeling pretty proud there for a while.

"Do something for Godsakes!" the mother yelled. "All you men sitting around, shit!"

And then she stood up and walked away. She took her rug with her, hung it over one shoulder like you've seen Indians do. It had designs of horses and trees on it. You could see that much when she stood there under the light of the porch. The light went off. I saw all the neighbors getting up. One came over and asked me why I just didn't do the thing a favor, put it to rest in peace.

After that, all that was left was Smith, myself, and my dog.

"Well, coyote expert," Smith said, "I say the dog's a coyote. Another thing I say is I say we get guns. I got a friend sells them secondhand and wholesale, and you'd be better off keeping that coyote of yours locked up and tied. Not many of us, if you haven't noted, have coyotes claiming to be dogs, roaming the neighborhood like they own it."

This may not be word for word exactly what the man said but it is about how he put it. I watched Smith take out a cigarette, bite off the filter, and spit it at my dog. I told Smith I did not think that was necessary of him to do.

"What?" Smith said. "You trying to talk?"

I do not fight much. You see my jaw, how it goes when I talk, and you see why. I just watched Smith walk away. His walk, like I said, those knees.

Wahoo was chewing Smith's cigarette butt. I kicked some dirt over the fire. I was kicking dirt when I heard Wahoo get up. The dog has to whine out a yawn to do anything, whatever, she does. I saw the coyote then. It was standing there like it wanted to know what we had cooking on the fire, I thought. Wahoo let out one of her gargled growls. I said to her, "Wahoo, sit, shut up." Her head was lowered, low to the ground. What there was of hair on her was raised from her neck down her back to her tail stub that was up. I had never knew her hair and tail could do that, go up like that. Both of them were standing there, coyote and dog, neither moving, just standing like they had some kind of signal going on. I picked up a log that had some fire on it, and threw it at our visitor. The coyote took one step back and went to smell at it. This is when Wahoo came charging in, dirt flying, into the coyote and the burning log. The two joined together at once. You could not tell whose ear was in whose mouth or whose leg was getting bitten on. They were tails, teeth, and paws. If there is one part I find not so pleasant to watch, it is how coyotes will fight it out to win the mate's prize. But this was my own dog fighting over nothing, no prize, it seemed to me, not even for the rights of property to someone else's backyard. In other words, I cannot begin to describe of it, of the sounds of dogs, or of how they did it, them rolling around, with me trying to break them up, taking a board with a nail in it and hitting one with it, hitting maybe both of them with it, I could not tell, and could not tell either which was the one that bit my arm. They just kept on, rolling into the playpen, and it turning over easy, them rolling along in the dirt, and eventually, finally into the fire that burnt them apart.

It got quiet then.

It was quiet for quite some time.

Wahoo lay on her side. The coyote, over there. There

seemed to be a good deal of blood around. You could almost smell it just by looking. I said, "Hey, Wah," and that coyote sprang up, shook like it had been in water, and ran out into the dark it had come from. Wahoo lifted her head, began doing some long licks from her chest down her leg to her paw. One of her ears looked like it was about to fall off. I was waiting for it to. I said to her, "Wah?" and went to pet her head. It was wet. I watched her lift herself, front legs first, up. Her back leg had something wrong with it. She would not set it down on the ground. I said to her, I said, "Hey, Wah!" The dog did not look up. She just turned, started doing this hop.

Following her, her sighs, grunts, and yawns, I was held to wonder who the victor or who the victim was—mate or prey, friend or neighbor, mother or child.

It was the dog that led the master home.

Way more fierce, these
edged-up walls, than pussy-
packed drained swim pool,
thinks Skate-Rat Lance, on
a finger-flip lip skid down
cement-wall riverbank.
"Fierce river, I am yours!"
shouts Skate-Rat Lance, riding on one hand when what

CHLORINE

is seen is a street-lean pack of Mexican duded-up bad in black, catching air off walls to bed flat where Skate-Rat Lance now stands, board in hand, thinking, Prick-ass beaners, this river, she is mine.

Skate-Rat Lance sees pack tail-fin stop, sees five shaved-up-side ball-bearing greased heads, asks, "You boys beginners?"

"Yes," says the one with crucifix stuck in nose. "We boys, we beginning to know how to make juice of white boy face."

"I'm talking tricks, man," says Skate-Rat Lance. "What tricks can you street meat not do?"

"Tricks," says the one with crucifix stuck in nose. "White boy, what you call tricks, we call dance. Sister Girl," says the one, "show white boy here your salsa dance."

Seeing Sister Girl roll boned-up shoulders loose, throw shaved-up head in swirl, jam black sleeves up silver-loaded arm, and push off pink board to fly up riverbank wall makes Skate-Rat Lance go into what he calls a fadeback sap to way back when Sister Laura, sweet Sister Laura, thinks Skate-Rat Lance, that filth was stuck all over you, your legs, your arms, your face, your goddamn good face. I swear to you, I did not mean to hurt you.

"White boy," hears Skate-Rat Lance, "you see that? Let's see you try what Sister Girl do."

Spaced out to the max, totally missed all that, thinks Skate-Rat Lance, dropping board on cement, saying, "I can out-thrash that."

One of the pack says, "Hey, boy, no pads."

"Yeah," says the one with arm slung over Sister Girl's neck, "get off your white-boy pads."

"Head pads, too," says another.

And taking pads off from wrists, from elbows, from knees, from head, Skate-Rat Lance thinks, That drop so deep, so fast, Laura, you hit so fast.

"Come on, white boy," says the one, "you white boys all so slow."

"Chill out, wetback," says Skate-Rat Lance, "this here is what I call the Death Walk Scratch," and with a push off one foot, Skate-Rat Lance shoots up riverbank wall, has one hand on wall, one hand on board, kicks sky, then tucks in tight to glide back down when front wheel snags rock and Skate-Rat Lance goes back on hands, on elbows, on head to a skinned stop on cement riverbed, where Skate-Rat Lance stays, thinking, Sister Laura, Sweet La, you throw me, you do, you can do this to me through and through.

When Sister Girl bends down over Skate-Rat Lance, Skate-Rat Lance sees Sister Laura, pulls her close, says, "Sister Laura, La, I swear, I do, I did not think a push would do that to you, you ran up behind, I saw your knees, your skirt, I thought a little push, you know, La, a little one, and there you went over and in, into that nasty, emptied pool."

"White boy, man, you dreaming something sick," says Sister Girl.

"White boy ate it bad, look at his head," hears Skate-Rat Lance.

"Get your beaner hands off me!" shouts Skate-Rat Lance. "Dumb-ass beaners, can't clean a pool, don't you know when you clean a pool you put a cover up over so no way sister falls in, dumb-ass, wetback beaners."

"Come on, white boy," says the one, lifting Skate-Rat Lance, "we got to get you somewhere."

In the arms of one with crucifix stuck in nose, Skate-Rat Lance sees cross over where Sister Girl is dug, and, "La," says Skate-Rat Lance, "you know that river where we go, that river so dry, what walls, La, riverbank walls so fierce, they are the killer most killermost walls no pussy I know, not even your brother, me, can ever beat, but say, La, tell me how you so small can carry me, where you take me, La, is there water?—water you and me, we can get down on our hands and knees and drink, tell me, La, tell me this, please, tell me there is water where you carry me."

TRICENTENNIAL

What Marsha likes best
about riding across the
country with her brother
Mickey in Mickey's pickup
truck is not so much how
many roadside animals her
brother Mickey has shifted
to Reverse to rerun over,
and then shifted to Stop to

strap roadside animals up on top of the flatbed roof of his pickup truck. Really, it is not so much how many times her brother Mickey has said to her, "Look, Mars, there's tons of food to feed your face off of, there, on the floor by your feet." Actually, what Marsha likes best is not mostly how crossing this country has taken two days and two nights to get from Richmond, Virginia, to this town Needles—Population 3, Elevation –9—California. No, what Marsha likes first and best, and this is really true, is getting to watch this Needles gas guy neck-lock her brother Mickey with a flat-tire jack, telling brother Mickey, "Nuh-uh, you're not going nowhere."

You see, when brother Mickey is led by flat-tire jack into the Needles Fill N Go gas station store, Marsha gets a chance to look at the test questions Mickey, in the last two days and nights, has written up on the back of the U.S. of A. road map that Mickey's kept rubberbanded to his side of the sun visor. Questions, Mickey has told Marsha, she will have to sit down and answer to be graded on by Mickey himself—A, B, C, D, E, F—once they reach the Save The Animals Commune their mother and father have been living at.

Mickey's no easy test-giver, no fifty-fifty shots here, Marsha sees, reading—

1. Name the state frog of Tennessee.
2. What state has the slowest-growing cow population?
3. In how many state(s) is the rabbit extinct?

Mickey has explained to Marsha that this test is to ensure that she, Marsha, won't grow up to be another moronic gutter slut like their other sister Michelle Ruth. That's Michael Bruce, their only other brother. Also known to Mickey as Bruth— Bruth who has not been let out of the flatbed of the pickup truck ever since he climbed up in two days and two nights ago.

Michael Bruce is lying on his side with a can of dog food held to his chest. Michael Bruce has held on to that can of dog food since dinnertime last night, at which time, while driving through Arkansas, Mickey was explaining to Marsha how these useless vagrants from Kansas had flocked their families down South to here, and, seeing what good farm land there was, they got down on their knees and shouted, "Kansas!" "Kansas!" they shouted. "This is *OUR* Kansas!" and that was how the state, get it, *AR*kansas was named. It was then, when Mickey was done telling Marsha this, that Mickey turned to look back at Michael Bruce, who had been banging that can of dog food against the glass between the flatbed and the front cab of the pickup truck since back at the Tennessee-Arkansas border. Michael Bruce pointed to the can of dog food, pointed to his mouth. Mickey reached under the seat, reached and waved the can opener at Michael Bruce.

Marsha takes Mother's all-vegetable lip crayon out of her shirt pocket, and, on the back of the U.S. of A. road map, writes—

1A. What state does not accept expired credit cards swiped from your own father?

Marsha has eyes that spot and name the breed of run-over roadside animals fenceposts ahead of brother Mickey who, back passing through the Oklahoma Wildlife Reserve, ran over twice—that's Reverse, Forward, Reverse, Forward—a torn tread of tire while Marsha, with her foot up on the dashboard, asked Mickey why he was wasting his good credit card gas on just another piece of bloodless nothing. With eyes like

Marsha has, she can see that there inside the Needles Fill N Go gas station store brother Mickey has taken off his C.S. of A., Confederate States of America, hat. Mickey scratches at his head, spits tobacco spit onto the floor and when the Needles gas guy puts the flat-tire jack up to Mickey's throat, Mickey takes a seat on the floor. Also, with eyes like Marsha's, every state license plate that is hanging on the gas station store wall can be read. There is LEI ME Hawaii, HOT BUNZ California, UTAH Utah.

And so on.

Question 4. In what state is General Robert E. Lee's horse buried?

Strapped on the roof of the flatbed of the pickup truck are Tennessee frog brains, an Arizona deer's head with eye intact, a dog neck with Texas dog tags, and a New Mexico roadrunner with no legs. Hung on the ice machine outside the gas station store there is a clock-thermometer that reads, 3:15, 112°. That's 3:15 a.m., SNT, Standard Needles Time.

Marsha wonders if there is enough air back there for Michael Bruce to breathe. Marsha wonders from 3:15 a.m. to 3:16 a.m. She knows how able Michael Bruce is at breathing in small, airtight spaces. All those times Michael Bruce rode in the parents' car trunk are paying off now. A year of all those times riding while brother Mickey drove Marsha and Michael Bruce to and from school, a year of Mickey signing field trip passes and school report cards, Mr. Mitchell Michaelson, Esq., III, above the Parent and/or Guardian dotted line.

Inside the gas station store Marsha sees the Needles gas guy talking on a telephone that is bolted to the license plate wall. The Needles gas guy has the telephone receiver held to his ear with his shoulder. With one hand he straightens a tilted license plate, with the other hand he holds the flat-tire jack down on brother Mickey's head. Brother Mickey spits.

Marsha writes—1AA. How many gallons of spit does it take to flood a town of Elevation −9?

Marsha smells a smell coming up from somewhere like what the family dog Melba used to ease out of itself on long car rides with every car window rolled up. Brother Mickey, in fact, took Marsha and the family dog Melba and Michael Bruce on one of those long car rides only days ago up into the Blue Ridge Mountains to go see the five side-by-side landmarks where they would all someday be lowered into next to Mo-maw and Po-paw Michaelson. When Mickey and Marsha returned to the car the family dog Melba was dead with the car windows rolled up, its head under the brake pedal. Brother Michael Bruce was alive with the car trunk closed, his head on the spare flat tire.

Burying the family dog Melba into his own landmark, Mickey told Marsha, "Remember, Mars, when I die, I want to be buried next to General Robert E. Lee's horse, Traveller."

Where the smell is coming from, Marsha smells, is from a sweaty plastic bag of year-old, nondairy, nonmammal breast o' chicken cheese pie Mother made before signing off: Once a week give Melba a spoonful of this yum-yum treat with her low-fat wheat grass juice. Mother's note is still taped on to the plastic bag. Marsha takes off Mother's note, tucks the note in her training bra for future forging reference of Mother's signature on credit card receipts, and throws the rest out of the pickup truck window.

A cat, with one leg in front and two legs in back, hops out from under the motor oil stand. This three-legged cat tears through the plastic bag with its front paw and eats at Mother's nondairy, nonmammal breast o' chicken cheese pie.

The writing of question 1AAA is interrupted by the Needles gas guy, who, shoving aside the three-legged cat with flat-tire jack, asks Marsha what she thinks she is doing. Just what, what does she think this is, some kind of, of a city dump?

Looking up close at the Needles gas guy, at the way his eyes go every which way but directly at where his mouth spits straight at her, Marsha thinks Mickey is right, this state is full of wet-brained vegetables slipped out West during the Great Continental Shift when so much gold knocked the country off tilt and every vegetable with a root for a brain slid over into what is known today as the Golden State of California.

"Mom and Dad are a result of the after-shift shock," Mickey explained.

"What's the delay over?" Marsha asks. "We've got an appointment, you know, a VIP appointment at oh eight hundred with top officials at the Save The Animals Commune."

"The STAC?" the Needles gas guy asks. "You mean, *the* STAC in El Antelope Valley?!"

"Wrong," Marsha says. "We're talking Big Bear, Big Bear Mountain, official headquarters."

"Really?" he says, swinging the flat-tire jack to golf club the three-legged cat. "Think I could jump a ride in the back?"

"Know the state frog of Tennessee?"

"Of what sea?"

"Sorry, no room," Marsha says, and hands him Mother's

credit card that she has kept bobby-pinned to her side of the sun visor. "Take this," Marsha says, "it's valid, here, look, I'll sign, give me something to sign, where'm I supposed to sign?"

The Needles gas guy is saying, "Gee, STAC" and "Gosh, STAC" as he runs the credit card through the credit card machine.

When Marsha sees brother Mickey stand up off the floor, she folds up the U.S. of A. road map and rubberbands it back on to Mickey's side of the sun visor. Mickey walks out of the gas station store zipping up his pants, grabs the neck of the three-legged cat that is chewing on Mother's nondairy, nonmammal breast o' chicken cheese pie and tosses the cat in with Michael Bruce in the flatbed of the pickup truck.

Marsha signs, Mrs. Martha Mitchell Michaelson, Esq., III, STAC, with STAC covering up the total cost of gas.

"Hey!" the Needles gas guy says, looking at the credit card. "Hey, this one expires tomorrow, you know?"

"Of course I know," Marsha says. "I know everything."

Driving away out of the Needles Fill N Go gas station, Marsha looks back and sees the three-legged cat has its head wedged between the can of dog food and Michael Bruce's chest. Marsha also sees the Needles gas guy is waving the flat-tire jack and, next to him, there is a girl who is waving, too, waving a license plate, NO PETS Virginia.

Question 1AAA—to be tended to by Marsha at a more convenient time—Name the two species of order currently populating the town of Needles, California.

Later, that's six test questions added on by brother Mickey later, added on while Marsha held the pickup truck steering wheel during the first ascent up Big Bear Mountain byway. That's one grizzly strapped on top of the flatbed roof later, grizzly, according to brother Mickey who, with the can opener, pried open the bear's mouth to see how the tongue— See, look, Mars, see how it moves when you give it a poke? You can always tell grizzlies by their innate ability to move their tongues when they're dead. And also, one failed attempt later by Marsha to read the six new test questions, when brother Mickey was restrapping those Texas dog tags from rattling on top of the flatbed roof. This, Mickey said, was for the sole benefit of Michelle Ruth who needs any slovenly beauty rest she can get. So this is how much later it is when Marsha sees SAVE THE ANIMALS COMMUNE o MI, which brother Mickey reads aloud as, "Give Me Anal Comanche O Me."

"I knew it'd be like this, didn't I tell you, Mars, it'd be like this, these inbred vegetables can't read, talk, or write right," Mickey says, and spits out the pickup truck window, and spit comes back in with the wind to hit Marsha upside the head.

"Say, Mars," Mickey asks, "what state did the Comanches come from?"

"We're here," Marsha says.

"I'll give you a hint, one hint," Mickey says, downshifting to Reverse, then upshifting to Forward. "Okay, the Comanches, now the Comanches played an important part in the death of that Yankee yellow-belly Custer—you know, Custer, the one that died of peyote indigestion."

"There's Mom," Marsha points. "I think that's Mom, doesn't that look like Mom?"

Mickey drives the pickup truck over a walking chicken, stops the pickup truck, says, "Where?" Says, "What are you pointing at? I can't see what you're pointing at. All I see is a dog, Mars, a fat old sheepdog taking a crap as big as Bruth's ass."

"Look behind it, you bat," Marsha says, "and tell me who that is. Tell me what other Mom scoops it, smells it, and then puts it in her backpack?"

"That's our Mom!" Mickey says, and drives the pickup truck into a hollowed-out tree trunk that has NONORGANIC WASTE painted on it.

Getting out of the pickup truck, brother Mickey asks, "Should we go over it again? Do you think we need to go over it again, again?"

"It" being the simple fact that credit cards, whether bought, stolen, or borrowed, do expire. "Expire" being a minor disturbance when there is no free cash around to fix the roof of the house back home that brother Mickey fell through while chasing raccoons with his portable sledgehammer. Raccoons to put, where else, but in Marsha's bed. In recent weeks of the fallen roof affair, raccoons have been scarce and brother Mickey has had to resort to lassoing Marsha's stuffed animals with curtain cords, to shutting Marsha's stuffed animals' heads in toilet seat lids, to sprinkling raccoon feces in Michael Bruce's dirty underwear drawer, and other such common acts of Parent and/or Guardian devotion to the gregarious extent that the family house is now something on the order of an Old Age Zoo where you can see tick farms locked in applesauce jars, see field mice nailed to walls by their tails with numbers chalked on their backs indicating their metric weight, and see, one cannot overlook, the ducks in the parents' whirlpool bathtub, ducks that have yet to be gutted and stuffed and sold to any one of the neighboring neighbors on the other side of the

Dominion State Parkway. With the new unexpired credit cards, brother Mickey has promised to purchase a brand new Michaelson, Esq., III, house complete with a live-in, Virginia-native, meat-cooking butler, which Mickey will pay for himself out of his own hard-earned pocket of credit cards.

Mickey, by the way, is twenty-three years old, well aware of his familial responsibilities.

"You go on," Marsha tells Mickey. "I've got to get out of this shirt—Mom would have a cow."

(This is another one of those popular shirts that on the front has a bunch of penguins being beat up with clubs by people in fur coats, that on the back has written ESKIMO S AND M.)

When brother Mickey goes on ahead, I-know-everything Marsha takes off her T-shirt, turns it inside out, puts it back on, and, most importantly, takes a look at the test questions.

5. In which eight states is the mockingbird the state bird?

6. In three words or less, explain the relationship between an armadillo and Amarillo, Texas.

7. Stop cheating!

Marsha writes—

1AAA. Why was General Robert E. Lee's horse, Traveller, buried in Harlem River, New York?

When Marsha hears Mother's Oh, child, Oh, my child, cry, Marsha folds up the U.S. of A. road map and rubberbands it back on to Mickey's side of the sun visor. Michael Bruce, Marsha sees, has moved from lying on one side to lying on the other side with the three-legged cat licking the inside of his ear, with the can of dog food held between his knees. Marsha hopes someday she will have a child to care for who is as easy to care for as Michael Bruce has been in these last two days and two nights.

And Marsha, by the way, is fourteen years old, well aware of her well-awareness.

Now there is Mother, Mother knocking on the pickup truck window, calling, "Sha, Oh, Sha, Sha-sha, love."

Marsha climbs out of the pickup truck, says, "Hi, Mom, so good to see you, Mom, Hi, Mom, so good to see you, Mom," as Mother's face with its pureed layer of papaya pulp and almond juice squishes up against Marsha's face.

"Oh," says Mother. "Oh."

And, "Oh," Mother says. "Oh, where's, where's Melba dog?"

"Mickey's grave," Marsha says.

"Home," Mickey says. "We left Melba home, someone had to feed Bruth."

"Bruth," Mother says. "Oh, Bruth, yes, Bruth."

The relatively repetitive "Ohs" of Mother are what brother Mickey has called a living example of the dwarfed vocabulary of Californians due, he hypothesized, to California's geographical proximity to that pathetic excuse for another United State—Hawaii—where people are pineapples barely able to manage a thirteen-letter alphabet. This case in point Mickey backed up with the one postcard Mother wrote during this last year, a postcard which read, "Hi, Oh, Hi, Oh, Bye, Bye-Bye, Aloha, Aloha Nui Loa."

Mother is looking, Marsha sees, holistically fashionable in her nonfiber T-shirt, with FREE THE SNAILS over the breasts, and a scarf tied around her hips, a scarf that looks to Marsha like someone vomited tomato, broccoli, and carrot curvy-saucy over it. Marsha also sees (with eyes as Marsha has, she has adapted for herself one swivel of a neck) that this Save The Animals Commune has chickens and goats and sheep and gerbils and even a spitting llama over there by that one and only tent. Up in the tree directly above where Mother is stuck on her "Ohs" there is a man who looks to Marsha like Po-paw Michaelson looked when he died riding a lawnmower-tractor that did not quite make it across the Dominion State Parkway, not quite enough in time for a sixteen-wheel gasoline truck to stop. This man looks like Po-paw Michaelson by the way he is hanging by one leg upside down from a tree same as Po-paw Michaelson hung by one leg upside down over the gasoline tanker of the sixteen-wheel truck, with Po-paw Michaelson's hand blocking WIDE RIGHT TURNS. The only difference with this man here, besides the obvious absence of the sixteen-wheel truck, is that this man is speaking, this man is saying, "Sing, birdie, sing-sing."

"Friend of yours?" Marsha asks.

"Oh, yes," Mother says. "Oh, one so aloha, yes."

Taking Marsha by one hand and Mickey by the other, Mother leads. "We go see Daddy," Mother says. "Go see Daddy, Oh."

Now in the some twenty-odd-bunk-bed, some two-hundred-fifty-five-animal (not including the mealworms in the mealworm-breeding canister brother Mickey kicked across the floor by pure accident) tent, brother Mickey and Marsha sit on the bottom bed of a bunk with Father. Father sits allowing

Mother to pick out fleas residing in the back hairs of his neck, Father allowing this leisurely repose after a workday of organizing official STAC reports for an impending snail petition.

Father speaks—

"Did you know that the snail, otherwise known as the gastropod mollusk, is the most populous terrestrial species in the State of California? Did you know that this terrestrial species, which travels by a muscular foot, conducts respiration, as you and I, through the exercise of membranous lungs? That this same species has developed antennalike eyeballs which can expand to a length of one-point-five centimeters, and can then retract to an immeasurable disappearance into its musculated head in less than point-one-nine-eighth of a second? That these absolutely evolutionarily unique beings can often live to be sixty human, that's you and me, sixty human years old, and yet! Yet, an estimated five-point-three million gastropoda, if you will, are being killed daily in the State of California by means of insidious garden pellets? That another, that's an estimated two-point-four million, are being stamped on daily by shameless children in driveways? That another twenty thousand are being boiled to death daily—picture yourself being boiled to your death, and then drowned in an all-dairy butter at some so-called eating establishment out in a town, for example, as Lost Angels. Do you kids, I don't think you kids do, do you kids realize that the loss of the gastropod mollusk, according to official STAC reports, may, can, and will lead to the extinction of our world as we know it today?!"

"Yes, sir, I did, sir," says Mickey.

"Daddy-da," says Marsha, "tell me more, please, tell me more."

And, "Oh," says Mother, "Oh, more, yes, more."

And so on goes the serenade of children in utmost need of what Father has, Father having the greater expense limit of the dual, Mr. and Mrs., credit cards, the card brother Mickey had termed the preferred card for pilfering ploys. And so on goes Mother, as well, Mother in utmost need of Father precisely where the hoard of fleas Oh so privately reside.

This moment being a brief testimony of Father's rampant testicles, rampant enough to generate the production of at least two lovingly grateful children who call out, "Yes, sir, sir," and "Daddy-da, more, please, tell me more!" This testimony being brief in so much as how long it takes Father to expound the virtues of extending the lifespan of not only our own God-forsaken country but of extending the universal lifespan of our own God-forsaken world via artificial snail insemination. As brief as it takes the man, who looked to Marsha like Po-paw Michaelson, to ladder, fall on the floor, and ladder his way up to the top bed of the bunk the family sits on, the man carrying a crow, the man calling, "Sleep, birdie, sleep-sleep." And also about as brief as it is for Mother to transport the thirty-eight fleas she has picked, named, and stored in a Band-Aid box and free them, "Oh, free," into the greater outdoors outside of the tent. Enough brevity already to enable Father to shut down those eyes of his, still speaking of snailhood extinction, and, speaking further of Michael Bruce, Father wanting to know if Michael Bruce has been mowing the parkway median strip as he has been so told to do.

"You can tell when Dad's talking in his sleep," Mickey says, "by how the flies shoot up into his mouth."

This, Marsha knows, is her cue. While brother Mickey

stands lookout for Mother at the tent's entrance, Marsha checks the most likely of places—Father's filebox, always kept, whether at home or away on business, tucked specifically under his bed. Marsha, with her head in Father's filebox, finds a nonessential, nongluten slice of celery pie, a photograph of Mo-maw Michaelson taking a whirlpool bath with the family dog Melba, a nonanimal prophylactic, and a joint savings, Mr. Mitchell Michaelson, Esq., III/Mrs. Martha Mitchell Michaelson, Esq., III, account book from the Commonwealth Bank of Virginia, the last entry reading July 3 (which was yesterday) a decline from $364.12 to $4.12.

$4.12!

When Marsha looked a year ago, the savings book read $3,588,963,842,754.86, Marsha, with her photographic mind, remembers. Marsha remembers, too, that in this same filebox there were ten flavors of credit cards to choose from. Ten was the exact amount to spread out the use of each credit card so thin as to go unnoticed by Father and Mother that purchases were indeed being made on Eskimo S and M shirts, on raids at the hamburger-cockroach stand at school, on stuffed animals in such a bountiful array that Marsha soon found herself crowded out of her own bedroom, having to sleep instead in brother Mickey's bedroom where tobacco spit hung from the ceiling beams, and most of all, on cash advances for the high-rising cost of having to hire brother Mickey to drive her up North to the Nation's Capital so she could scrape post-pre-war moss off Abraham Lincoln's legs for a biology project at school.

$360.00!

What, Marsha thinks, another mastectomy for a mangy rat?!

Even Michael Bruce's circumcision, surgically performed by Father himself (Father: one more to add to the list of failed bankers turned veterinarian-podiatrists) only cost a mere $4.99 plus Virginia State Commonwealth Tax. Even, even the newly amended United States Constitution, printed on biodegradable, noneatable paper, framed in red, black, and blue plastic to hang above the fireplace back home, did not cost that much. And the cost for that, Marsha remembers, included the price for having it shipped across Korea, South America, and the Atlantic, taking only three years for it to arrive at the Michaelson front doorstep, arriving complete with typographical errors Marsha was quick to correct—that all animals are not crated but *created* equal, that all animals are endowed not by their crater but by ther *creater* with certain *inanimate* not inalienable rights, that among these rights are the rights to life, liberty, and the pursuit of *sappiness* not happiness.

(It might as well be added that this Constitution was a bona fide deluxe version with a microfilmed signature of a former president of the United States, a president who brother Mickey had once described as a non-American inmate born in that prison city of New York, a prison which brother Mickey once said ought to be bombed off the face of this planet by someone with the comparable grace of John Wilkes Booth.)

Marsha hears from above her squatting position, above Father's fly-catching snore, that the man in the bed above is singing that boring morning song you are ordered to sing at the start of every school day with everyone looking around at everyone else to see who is actually making the effort to sing about how fruited the Incidental Plains once were. This sort of attempt at song, courtesy of the Po-paw Michaelson look-alike, has got the crow crowing, and Father, his head fallen back over the bedpost, is thy-hooding animalhood in his singing-sleep.

In comes brother Mickey now, carrying the grizzly over his shoulder, with Mother following, petting the grizzly's head, calling, "Oh, Daddy, Daddy, come see." Marsha puts the joint savings account book into her training bra, the book being an unsuitable bra-stuffer for a well-aware fourteen-year-old girl, and pushes the filebox under the bunk bed.

"Who am I?" wakes Father.

"Here you are, sir," says Mickey, unloading grizzly off his back and onto the bunk bed. "Saved this one myself," Mickey says. "Sir, you cannot conceive of the jungle it is out there. Beyond these barracks savage men and women are axing defenseless creatures left, right, and left, and I thought perhaps, sir, you, with your patented resuscitation methods, could revive this victim from its mild stupor."

"Good work," says Father.

"Oh, I," says Mother, "I wish, I wish I were a roo."

Quick translation: Prior to Mother's California existence, Mother often explained how in her next life she hoped to be a kangaroo so that she could tote her children along with her in the furry-warm of her tum-tum pocket. Oh, where went the days when Mother could talk in four-syllable words, when Father could maintain at least a quadruple-digit savings account figure?

"Daddy-da," says Marsha, taking a seat on Father's lap, fingering the hairs on Father's chest. "Brilliant brother Mickey has an idea that we, Mickey and me, I mean, excuse me, sorry, Mickey and I, that Mickey and I will drive this country from sea to shining sea in search of naughty people who axe to death poor animals, and Daddy-da, brother Mickey and I have only crossed Interstate 40, and there are more than a thousand more interstates, byways, highways, freeways, tollways, tunnels, bridges, and camp trails left to cross, and Daddy-da, could we, do you think we could maybe, you could maybe, like, temporarily, like, lend us your STAC credit card to pay for the gas it will take to fulfill our MTSONUG, Mission To Save One Nation Under God?"

"Oh, God," says Mother, "God is dog."

"You could write it off on your expense account," adds brilliant brother Mickey.

"Swell idea," says Father, peering under the grizzly's eyelid. "But there's a problem you kids unfortunately haven't considered, and that is that credit cards are made with protective porcupine spines, and accordingly, us local STACites have boycotted the use of such materials. Another problem you've overlooked is that money, as you must know, is trees and trees are money. What do they teach you in school these days anyhow? How could you kids not possibly know that the more we randomly slaughter our trees, the more animals, such as the Wyoming woodpecker, will have no place to home their peckers. How would you, son, feel if one day you awoke to find that that dear home you'd been pecking your pecker in had suddenly, without warning, vanished? You'd be one homeless bird, now wouldn't you, son?"

"So what you're saying, then," shouts Mickey, "is that you're going to turn your back on your only son?"

"It troubles me to hear you think like that," says Father, "but if that's how you choose to look at it, well, then, yes, yes, I guess that's how it stands."

"Get your hands off my grizzly!" Mickey shouts. "That's *my* grizzly, I found it and it's *mine!*"

"For people mountained majesties," sings the Po-paw Michaelson look-alike.

"Go screw a tractor!" yells Marsha.

"Marsha!" shouts Father, "show some respect! This man carries a Du Pont pedigree as old as the Delaware state he was born in!"

"He can go die there, too," Marsha says.

"Oh, no, bad," says Mother, "bad, Oh, bad, bad, bad."

What's a family to do?

Brother Mickey takes the grizzly by the fat of its neck and pulls the grizzly off the bed, shouting, "We made meatloaf out of Melba and your daughter Michelle Ruth devoured every bit of it!"

Marsha pulls off the Eskimo S and M shirt, flings it at the parents, yells, "Merry Christmas!" and follows the grand departure of brother Mickey.

Father tends to Mother, who holds the shirt to her eyes, Father telling Mother, "Now, now, there, there, it's all right, they're gone now, they're going now, there they go."

As with most family disputes of this nature, this last one was reminisced about years later by brother Mickey, a.k.a. the Honorable Mitchell Michaelson, Esq., IV, President of the Re-United States as he sat in the renovated triangle office of the White House. The Honorable President reminisced with his sister Marsha, Secretary of Treasury, while she counted the three hundred-dollar bills remaining from post-pre-war days, the three hundred-dollar bills she calculated to equate to a total value of three buffalo nickels. The reissuing of the buffalo nickel was a birthday present the Honorable President gave to Father on Father's deathbed as a part of the State of the Union address which was broadcast live, worldwide. Father died of flea infestation only days after Mother died of the epidemic Oh So Cal Flu, its primary symptoms involving a slow disability of speech and thought patterns.

Well aware of the decline of his familial responsibilities now that Mother and Father had died, buried in their respective landmarks aside Mo-maw and Po-paw Michaelson, the family dog Melba, and brother Michael Bruce who, upon hearing the victorious reelection results of his unopposed brother, buried himself alive in his own landmark, never to be heard from again; at any expense, these familial concerns no longer weighing upon his moral conscience, the Honorable President was able to devote his heartfelt time to other international causes. These causes were those such as transporting General Robert E. Lee's horse, Traveller, to a site on the White House lawn; recommencing the production and distribution of credit cards so that no American child would have to suffer the psycho-economic traumas the Secretary of Treasury and the Honorable President had to undergo in their innocent youth; freezing, on a daily basis, the President's honorable spermatozoa and then sealing these spermatozoa in a vault located adjacent to a methane tank in the Pentagon basement, this so that Michaelson genes could be carried on for one more generation; assigning the Du Pont pedigree man to carve the Honorable President's head in with the other stone heads at Mount Rushmore (this was Mother's deathbed wish, relayed in Hawaiian hula sign language). And lastly, under oath to his faithful constituents, the Honorable President swore that before the end of his fourth term in executive office, he would devise a test, a mandatory test on the history of the Re-United States for each and every American of each and every age to take, to answer, to be graded on by none other than the Honorable President himself. Faithful to the oath, this grade would then serve as the prime factor the Honorable President would have to determine who is, and, more importantly, who is not a worthy citizen of the Re-United States. This the Highly Honorable President professed was one step for Americankind, one step to preserve, for centuries to come, what our forefathers lost their lives for, for one nation, above God, divisible, with liberty and justice for all.